CW00765734

A NEARLY MURDER

A Nearly Murder © 2023 Timo Savimaki.
All Rights Reserved.

No part of this book may be reproduced in any form or by any electronic or mechanical means including information storage and retrieval systems, without permission in writing from the author. The only exception is by a reviewer, who may quote short excerpts in a review.

This book is a work of fiction. Names, characters, places, and incidents either are products of the author's imagination or are used fictitiously. Any resemblance to actual persons, living or dead, events, or locales is entirely coincidental.

Printed in Australia
Cover and internal design by Shawline Publishing Group Pty Ltd
First Printing: July 2023

Shawline Publishing Group Pty Ltd
www.shawlinepublishing.com.au

Paperback ISBN 978-1-9229-9347-2
Ebook ISBN 978-1-9229-9358-8

Distributed by Shawline Distribution and Lightningsource Global

A catalogue record for this work is available from the National Library of Australia

More great Shawline titles can be found by scanning the QR code below.
New titles also available through Books@Home Pty Ltd.
Subscribe today at www.booksathome.com.au or scan the QR code below.

A NEARLY MURDER

TIMO SAVIMAKI

To Di, of course.

*I would like to acknowledge invaluable advice from
my mentors Janine Johnston and Bob Leschen at
'Rendezvous to Write', a program run by Hawthorn
Community House in Melbourne. Likewise, I am grateful
to Lisa Ferguson, fellow student at Spanish school.
I appreciate their time taken to read the text forensically
and constructively. Finally, thank you to Dot Leitner,
a classmate from high school days, who was first to read
the manuscript and keep my feet on the ground.
Finally, thank you to granddaughter Rory Toghill for
her creative interpretation of the main character,
Mary Chiaprisi.*

*This book is a work of fiction dusted with fact.
Incidents and names and characters are the products
of imagination, and any resemblance to real persons is
purely coincidental. For authenticity some events
are historically correct, but interpretation and errors
are mine alone.*

Mary must have had some Latina bloodlines, judging by her colouring and dress sense. She never simmered. She was quick to anger, but just as quick to pass that squall.

A consummate actor, she could project submission when it suited. She would hold out her hand, a little limp, unlike her firm business handshake. She would flash just the briefest smile and its twin, the dimple. There was still another dimple in reserve. Then she would lower her head ever so slightly, put nervous on her face, and tremble her handbag to the floor.

Contents

Prologue

A Bout of Mortality

Easy Pickings

Horse Talk

Mary Chiaprisi

Legal Eagle

Slow Boat

The Articled Clerk

Hiding in Plain Sight

There's a Bridle Hanging on the Wall

The Auctioneer

The Plight of the Unicorn

Dance the Tarantella

Death in Paradise

The Entrepreneur

Dark Clouds in Jindabyne

Where There's a Will There's a Way

The Brittens, Wilson, and Finnbar Mahoney

The Judge's Associate

The Funerals

Tom Dooley and TwoBoots

Paxton and Prey

Merton and the Brittens

Softly Softly

I am Woman

Pity the Plod or, 'Murder she Cried!'

Jindy Digs

In the Lion's Den

Encore

The Big Man

Back in the Lion's Den

TwoBoots

The Awakening

The Next Move

Quaff a Mudgee Red

Boot Pressure

The Big Man Part Two

Revelation

Wilson to Merton, Over and Out

Showdown

The Will

There are no Winners

Denouement

Loose Ends

Epilogue

Prologue

A story seeing daylight in the year twenty twenty-three but set around sixty years earlier creates a contradiction. For the writer who lived those times, it's a simple dredging of the mind. On the other hand, younger reades can absorb the dated story only through the prism of their social norms.

It's valid. Just read on and judge as you will. The settings are accurate. Southeastern New South Wales and its towns are for real, lived in, fact-checked, and all. The same goes for Perth and Sydney. Mid-western NSW is pure fiction, as are all the characters.

The events in Jindabyne could have happened, but of course did not. Female heroes at that time – not likely. That is a today construct. Macho males put in their place by women – not then. It is so today, thus no need to suspend your disbelief. Just for fun, accept it, lock stock and spoof.

The quoted verses are redolent with the emotions of that instant. That's why they are there. It doesn't matter that they may be in the future. Just dream on and time shift. The story will be all the better for it.

A Bout of Mortality

'The child is the father of the man'

William Wordsworth

Tom Dooley feared that the bastardry of his life would catch him some time. He was born over a grave. We all are.

He showed his future colours from his first days of school. Artful dodger is an apt description of young Tom. He wheedled someone else to do whatever he didn't want to do. He would slink under a desk instead of helping the other kids tidy up after craft. If the teacher caught him at it, his reply was always that he was grabbing craft scraps from under there. In fact, there was nothing ever under the desks. Craft was always done at the craft table.

He was last in line in the emu parade that picked up playground rubbish. He hardly picked up anything. Why would you when the other kids were happy to do it all? Especially if you whimpered. He hid his cunning nature by looking adults in the eye, charming them with bright eyes and a broad smile, innocence itself.

If he were Buddhist, there would be no future for him. He had never practiced a single step on the middle path to nirvana. He bled others for his own gain.

As a Hindu, the bad karma in his circle of life would bring him back as a grub. Hindus conceive of time as a circle. You can rotate it at any time to explore the present, unencumbered by the future or the past. This story dwells in the mind, its remembering fluid, its telling just another hour on the clock. If at times the result appears incongruous, reposition yourself wherever and accept the lightheartedness of it all. Just shift yourself around your mental time dial to make it work. After all, we are not bothered that electrons can't have a definite position and direction of motion at the same time.

Tom's Christian self would have only a slim hope of reaching the afterlife, more likely burn in hell. What happens to a total heathen like Tom? He too had to put his foot somewhere, this way or that, any way but not no way, surely. Redemption? Or resignation? Or condemnation? Tom was caught. How could he repay what he had borrowed from his future?

We are all born over our graves. Our start and finish lines are all in the same place. How many people know that? It's what happens in between birth and death that matters. Nobody fears that previous time and place where you hovered for an eternity. Your parents released you from that one through their act of love. You did the same for your kids. Still, we fear the next eternity, quite forgetting that we had survived a previous one. Rituals, superstitions, and religions have been invented to make the prospect – dare one say it – inviting?

What were Tom's debts to society? It was smooth if devious sailing until he was thirteen. Then a shadow sailed over his moon. The devil poked him with his pitchfork. Yesterday's rainbow bird turned into a raven. Tom was done. Hang down your head, Tom Dooley.

Easy Pickings

Eva Rumford was a sweet young thing. Tom Dooley was a handsome boy, charming to a fault. Life lit the fuse to their juvenile hormones, right on cue. Their age of innocence was drawing to a close. They started to know everything. In their pubescent mindsets, their parents started to know less and less.

No jukebox played any danger signal inside their 1950s heads. Maybe only the top eight hits registered. And then Tom would take his lawnmowing money down to the record shop with Eva. Together they would flick along the vinyl offerings. It was quick and easy, as the discs were arranged in sections by genre and alphabet. The music their parents listened to was in fuddy duddy corner, away from pop. Rock and roll came along with Bill Haley. Crooners like Frank Sinatra, jazz, classical – yuk.

Big was better, but Tom could never afford full-sized albums. Too much diameter, too, for that old record player of his. For Tom, those 45s were more affordable in summer. That was busy season for the lawnmower. Tom could even afford to shout Eva a spider drink in the Greek café. The best was creaming soda with a scoop of vanilla ice cream on top and raspberry flavour concentrate spilled over. Once halfway, the drink straw mushed what was left. That bubbling pink was perfect to relish off a long-handled spoon. Then it was off to the record shop.

Kids will be kids. Boys, feet laden with mysterious teenage smell-hormone, were the worst. Their shoes had to live outdoors when not on feet. Mums saw to that. Mums were not to be messed with. Boys were loud, pushy, strong enough to hurt, weak enough to avoid older boys. Not wise enough to learn the obvious. Some hung out with girls, like Tom did. Most hung out in obnoxious boy gangs. Tom also hung out with boys who swaggered just as he did. They egged each other on, and society did not always agree with the outcome. Neither did parents and police. It seems nothing ever changes. We see that this is still so, a quarter way through century twenty-one.

One of Tom's swagger pals had lots of 45s at home. He didn't even mow lawns or wash cars or do a paper run. What the? Eddie Murray just gave a sly wink. Tom's jealousy knew no bounds. He decided to follow Eddie's example.

Eva was his first recruit. She swished into the long seat at the Greek cafe, backing on another such bench, separated from it by a high, brown, polished plywood panel, with big tables completing the dining settings. The booths stretched the length of the sidewall, punctuated by the side entrance. Eva's swish came from her long white coat, the one with the big inside pocket. She had sewn that herself. The creaming soda spider never tasted so good. The sugar hit was good for bravery and bravado as well.

Tom selected the fast-rising number seven from the top eight hits, and took it to the counter, mower money in hand. The till was at right angles to the counter. That way there was some room on the counter to place purchases. That counter was not very big. Neither was the record shop. The distraction was complete. Eva joined Tom to complete his transaction. They walked out, Eva with a flat reinforcement where the secret pocket was. When they got to the park, Tom invited Eva over to listen to the top of the pops that came out of that pocket.

A long journey starts with the first step. For Tom, not for Eva. She stopped after a few such expeditions, as her upbringing caught up with her. The thrill was not strong enough to overcome the guilt.

Grandparents learn so much from their kids. When the next generation comes into their purview, grandpa knows what that child will be like in later life. Grandma does even better with her female intuition. Mum and dad not so much. They are too busy acquiring their own knowledge about human pups. The grandparents judged correctly that Eva had admirable qualities of honesty and a sense of fairness. Her face was an open book. It lit up like a beacon with anger or surprise or confidence or disappointment or embarrassment. Other kids have antennae too, and they were pulled into Eva's orbit because of the empathy that she exuded.

Small wonder then that Tom's behaviour generated sufficient velocity to escape from Eva's gravity. He was so self-centred that he never noticed that he was being flung into outer space. His triumph was, 'Always get someone else to do your dirty work for you.' That became his mantra of life. No use advising him to listen to his conscience. His inner voice was an arsehole. That rubber never hit the road. If ever he wrestled with his conscience, and that's doubtful, he never lost. His life was never ravished by virtue. He talked so much he could break an auctioneer.

As a baby he must have been rocked all wrongly, his potty training all askew, perhaps even dropped on his head.

Horse Talk

'There was movement at the station,
For the word had passed around
That the colt from Old Regret had got away
And joined the wild bush horses – he was worth a thousand pounds,
So all the cracks had gathered to the fray.'

Banjo Paterson

Today's savvy youth could easily date Martin O'Hanlon without carbon dating: he ate his meals without first photographing them on a mobile. And by the clothes that he wore every day. Who's that western dude then? Long and lean, his face hide tanned by too much sun, he rocked as he walked with bowlegs that you could drive a horse through. That is how he got them in the first place, or should that be, over years astride one. Spurs tinkled in his head, his tinnitus. He snuffled as he ate, like the beasts he loved so.

On the rare occasions that a roll-your-own durry did not droop from his lips, as he rocked evenings to 'n' fro on his chair suspended on arcs, there was an inadvertent nostril whistle and a snail trail of chin dribble. He wore lazy stubble before it became fashionable. Unruly nose hairs vibrated in sympathy and tickled. From time to time he had to scratch them. Momentarily that put paid to the whistle that his wife hated so. As did she his tobacco breath and brown bent teeth. She seemed not bothered as Martin got sick. And sicker.

Jennifer née Spring wondered what in the world had she been thinking that 1959 spring day in Jindabyne, when she said, 'I do.' She mused that she must have thought that any man who loved horses must love her the same. Any man who whispered sweet nothings in a horse's ear, patted it lovingly, fed it daily with nothing but the best, scraped the post-hosing warm water off it even when it had not been ridden that day, made sure its feet were shod with the best shoes that farrier kingdom could produce, that called in the equine tooth fairy twice a year just to make sure, such a man would love her too. That was then. This was now.

She had adored horses. Then. Not now; they were too much competition. It didn't take long for her to realise that after the horse, there was no love left over for her. On the contrary, he expected to be treated like he treated his horses. And had made it perfectly clear that the horse came first, that she was last in a very big horse field, if she were a horse. Which she wasn't. That made her all but invisible to him. He did look good on a horse's back. Upright he sat astride his mount as he rode it like a ramrod. But his grace dismounted at workday's end, posture compromised by a stoop. With him around, the house was steeped in horse dung smell.

She snapped into his clear focus for any perceived mistake: eggs not fried just so, the bacon not crackling crisp enough at the rind, any hint of cancer-inducing burn on his toast, and coffee in his favourite mug at not precise steaming hot. Two sugars, and served at exactly five a.m.. After all, there was a lot of horse-whispering to do that day.

About eight years into this match made in hell, Jen went to Jindabyne's only solicitor, Lasseter & Co. She stated her business. Harry L raised his shaggy, unruly, over-eighty-year-old right eyebrow, revealing a pale blue, intelligent, not unfriendly, rheumy eye. The other eye was all but hidden by a drooping, uncouth, left side, ungroomed brow mess. He was still spry. He sat down to pee but still was able to stand on one leg to pull on his underpants. Weekends he hiked the bush, shorter tramping now than before.

Without comment Harry set about fulfilling her request. Business not so brisk, he volunteered to do it on the spot. Jen watched his splotchy, black-veined, long-fingered, nail-manicured hands write out a proforma for her, sign and stamp it. 'There, it's done.'

Job over, he let his right eyebrow migrate south, back into place, and his head resumed the look of a walrus half asleep on some rocky winter beach, with a droopy moustache.

Jen had a short chat with the receptionist at front office on the way out, paid, and threw the receipt into the bin in the street. Skiing would soon change that hamlet forever. She extracted the precious document and burned its Lasseter envelope in the fireplace. She put the form in a plain envelope with her birth certificate and ditto marriage, and hid it in her secret place. She didn't want Martin to see that signed and Lasseter-sealed document with its legal title, 'Change of Name by Deed Poll'. It requested a change to Mary Flamboya. He had noted her birth certificate details. It was a bit unusual, but Harry's lips were sealed.

Martin had enjoyed his wedded bliss for one half-score years – felt like of a full score to Jen – when Martin met Eva Rumford's former classmate Tom Dooley. It was a fitting match, shifty, swaggering Tom up to his amoral tricks, and the bow-legged man from Snowy River, well-honed in selling dodgy horses. It did not matter that they were not even his own. He never told Jen that.

She found out about that *officially* when the Jindabyne constabulary came calling in early 1969. It did not come as a surprise; she already suspected, but had said nothing, had known nothing, had feigned surprise, and was not called as a witness at Martin's horse thief trial. Banjo could well have had a Tom and Martin in mind as he penned his iconic poems about the goings-on in the bush.

Martin O'Hanlon got six months at Her Majesty's pleasure in the Cooma lockup, good-behavioured after four. Tom Dooley got none. He made sure that he had hired someone else to do his dirty work. Eddie Murray had taken the place of Tom's first apprentice, the beautiful Eva Rumford, from all those years ago. Get others to do your dirty work.

For Jen that sentence was manna from heaven. She was nobody's servant now. Freed slave. What's the feminine of freeman? She was clever too, though Martin was too thick to know that. Horses had drugged and stupefied his any empathy toward fellow man. Closest woman too. By the time he got out, she would be gone. She let it be known she was off to Bega to stay with an aunt.

She packed a big case with clothing essentials. That still left a couple of drawers full of tired, jaded garments fit for no woman. There was no lace, nothing pretty, nothing for best, no hat, only a beanie minus its pompom. Not that the big case contents were much better.

Quickly she took one last cruise around the stables, the tool shed, the tack room, the feed shed. At the back of the round yard, the farther side from the road, Jen absently picked up a notebook, black, covered in sawdust and dried horse dribble. She slapped it against her bum on the way back to the house. It too went into her shoulder bag, her survival kit, full of things that menfolk do not know and wives do not tell. In the haste of it all, 'rummage bag' would be a better description. Over the coming months, essentials rose to the surface, and things that might come in handy one day gradually sank, the notebook with them.

She had already gotten rid of their stock of horses at heavily bargained prices. Cash only. No duplicates of written receipts.

No names and addresses. There was no record left behind to show that the horses had even been sold. Maybe they had just run away to the bush brumby herds from whence they had come. Bugger Martin, he would just have to go and catch some more once he got out.

Jen stuffed the shoulder bag with crisp new bank notes, lots of them. As she had never received any mail, there was no address of hers to cancel at the Post Office. No forwarding address. No bank account to close. Martin had been the dole-master. There were no tracks of hers anywhere. The only papers she packed along with the dollars with Caroline Chisholm's head on them were in her plain envelope. She would need those for divorce proceedings (if necessary) and name change (tick).

She also very carefully packed a sizeable suede leather pouch with draw strings, into that shoulder bag. It held quite a collection of her grandmother's jewels, bequeathed to her. Grandma came from a wealthy grazing family, and Mum had said that these stones are your security if you ever need to call on them. Never ever tell anyone you have them. They are your business.

Jen pictured Martin splashing cold water on his face, shaving it every once in a while, and then cooking breakfast for himself and brewing coffee, precise specifications forgotten. Unable to blame anyone else, he would just have to eat his own fare, without demur, without complaint, without retribution, though he would know that he would never qualify for a job at any café in town. She smiled to herself and hoped that Martin would still have enough energy left to go cuddle his horse.

Mary Chiaprisi

Mary Chiaprisi. Jen didn't know where that new name came from. She just invented it. By a fluke, Chiaprisi is a Sicilian hamlet of very few inhabitants.

Like musical notes carousing, Jen's dark flashing eyes matched her always tanned complexion and newly-returned vivacious smile. All she had ever wanted to do was ride horses. All that got her was a dreadful husband. Thereafter, smiles had little to do with her face. It had matched the daggy clothes she had been forced to wear.

Jennifer Spring must have had some Latina bloodlines. Trouble was, there was no stud book to certify the sires and dams in her breeding. But how else to explain her colouring, her explosion into whatever mood struck her? She never simmered. She was quick to anger, and just as quick to pass that squall. She had trouble standing still, her hands as expressive as her vivacious face, and shoulders shrugging, slumping, sagging and uplifting in concert with her mood.

She didn't just put one hand over her mouth when embarrassed, she used both, and visibly grew smaller in her vain attempt to disappear altogether. And when she was dismissive – she took a step back, arched from the waist likewise, and twirled her forefinger in circular motions to nor-west of her shoulders. She was charm personified.

Now she was coloured Mediterranean. She eschewed the dowdy of her marriage garb for a bit of colour, glitz and style. Her dress and her nature were now as one. She didn't just walk.

She danced as though she were in the *Sound of Music*. She flashed her pearly whites a lot. She waved her hands as she spoke, a lot. Her dimples enchanted, a lot. She enjoyed the company of the men and women, who treated her as one of their own in the Italian Club of West Perth. Jennifer Spring-O'Hanlon had simply disappeared, in person and persona. Mary Chiaprisi emerged like a beautiful butterfly from a chrysalis.

As the new Mary prospered, so the old unchanging Martin just endured. What you did when you were young keeps you company when you are old. Martin steadily grew sicker. His tomorrows were closed for business. This had been going on for quite a long time. He still talked to the horses and engaged in horse talk with other men. Buyers were now wary of his reputation and were much tougher customers of his than they were of any other horse trader. Martin endured the ostracism until it, too, gradually wore away. Bit by bit they learned that Martin was no crook. He had only had a crooked friend, who had conveniently disappeared once the victim had been scammed. Or so they thought.

His body took aging very badly. He that mighty youthful horseman now hobble-walked into premature middle age. 'Me 'orse bucked me off, right leg broke to pieces. Bloody 'ell.'

With it came premature rheumatism, lumbago, sciatica, neuralgia and peripheral neuropathy. His health got worse. Nothing inside his head ever changed, stuck there from the beginning. Funny then that from time to time he missed Jen. It had no effect on him. Or did it?

In April 1970, Martin died. Why oh why, Jen, had you not just waited? New Mary did not cry when she saw the death notice in the *Sydney Morning Herald* that she always bought two weeks old, road-delivered to Perth.

She deeply regretted that her love of horses had blinded herself to herself. She had thought that horses were life itself. If only she had waited, before falling for Martin's horsemanship, mistaking it for love

of the man. After only a few weeks under the same roof, she saw
clearly what she had done. Her quality of introspection burst into life
that instant. She heaved a sigh of relief that the ruin of her life had
departed, this time for good. She vowed in that instant to make good
the rest of her life. She began preparing herself for something new
over the hill.

Legal Eagle

'Up to me neck in Moola Moola mud

Up to me neck in water

Up to me neck in Moola Moola mud

South of the Queensland border'

Shearers' song

Finnbar Mahoney, always known as Finn, originating from County Kerry, Ireland, small town lawyer, did what small town lawyers everywhere do. Conveyancing, wills, estate administration, divorce, defending minor criminals, setting up company structures, presiding over a local club or two, owning a fair slab of the town, and generally friend of the well-to-do. Unlike them though, he intimately knew the rest of the townsfolk, through his work. All the same he didn't drink with workmen. The Moola Club was not where men in workwear went.

He was big and tall and handsome, still carrying the musculature of a man in his prime. From his skin, a single bristle high on his cheekbone was centred on a faint mole. Male beauty spot, you might say.

He met his kind in the club where members could afford the annual dues, white collar professionals all. None was prone to gossip. They were duty bound not to disclose clients' confidences. Doctors, lawyers, dentists, bankers, men all, were bound by their professional codes which they stringently followed. Where confidential boundaries intersected, they consulted in their offices.

There wasn't enough talking power in the world to persuade Finn to talk about his work at the club. Loose lips would soon staunch the flow of butter to his bread. And yet he was gregarious in that easy manner so typical of the Irish, with life seen through the prism of humour. He knew by training when to hold his tongue, unnatural as that felt.

He harboured a deep sorrow from his past, a love cut short at the height of its promise. He never spoke about it to anyone. No one could possibly have guessed from his demeanour. Cheerful to a fault, polite with all, no matter their station in life, he treated every person like a person, no pre-judging by occupation or wealth. His adopted small outback hometown was not awash with eligible young women, and that suited him perfectly. He threw himself into work instead of grieving.

As a result the good citizenry of that town found him hard to get to know well. They thought him perhaps as a bit aloof. As soon as they got close, he would employ some witticism or other to make himself appear lightweight, which he certainly was not. Only to the more observant did it seem he was hiding pain behind this humour.

He socialised as an adjunct to his work, not as a part of normal life. In truth, his work was his life, and it suited him perfectly to have a work social life instead of a social life. Behind that persona that he cultivated was a much more complex human being. He was cultured, well read, highly educated but chose not to show it, loved the arts but was able to appreciate only one art form in this backwater. That was Aboriginal art, and he soon became immersed in its manifestation under the sandstone overhangs by the river.

He couldn't get enough of the stories that the elders were happy to share with him, especially when he started writing a book about them. Dreamtime stories became his fixation. Deep friendships with the local tribe resulted. Finn had found substitute happiness. He became a collector.

Nonetheless, occasional gossip did circulate around Finnbar's club. The real estate agent was privy to many a client's affairs, private and otherwise. Such knowledge was natural stock-in-trade, necessary if you were to successfully match a desirable property to available means. No tyre kickers please. Lawyer and agent were Siamese twins, sharing common client and privy to his financial stress test imposed by the banker. In the club you could not gossip about such people. But human nature will have its way. No idle chatter until the drastic happened – a divorce, contested Will, too many domestics, thus courtroom appearances, all reported in the local rag.

From time to time, graziers would descend on the club. The season's wool clip delivered, they came to town with their such-brimmed hats, five-pocket moleskins, thick-woven light blue grazier shirts, and de rigueur burnished RM Williams comfort craftsman boots.

No rouseabout ever donned that uniform, never saw the inside of that club. They got pissed in the public bar of the Royal George and left their spare cash with the starting price bookie. Somehow the SPs were known to all, except for some mysterious reason, not to the local boys in blue. Without WhatsApp or Facebook, without fail, on that town's one-day-a year race meeting at the local track, you couldn't find them at the pub. They had just evaporated. Twenty-first century Apple Mac intelligence would run a distant last in that field.

The legit bookies at the track, with their Gladstone bags full of paraphernalia, spivvy quasi-brimmed porkpies with broad colour-blind hat bands, looking for all the world like the proverbial pox doctor's clerk, never faced SP competition that day. The scrawny chalker scribbled up the odds on a blackboard, as the mathematician bookie worked out his odds according to the flow of punts. The punter dreamed of making a killing, even as the bookie calculated the basis for a near-sure profit.

The punter was backing his single sample of the field. The bookie was an innate statistician. He was probing the shape of the money probability curve of the total horse population of that race. He was shaping that curve to his advantage, by altering the odds of each horse as punters' money descended on it. A grazier and a rouseabout seen together with the paddock bookmakers – now that's a double no bookie would ever touch.

Finn practised in a western town half a day's drive from Sydney towards Adelaide, on the banks of the Moola Moola, an Aboriginal name for precious waters or something like that. The town was simply called Moola, same as Wagga Wagga is shortened to just one guttural sound. Moola is also Aussie slang for money. Apt. At the time of the Korean War, a little before the time that we are talking about, wool was selling for a pound a pound.

The graziers were rolling in Moola, you could say. Is that a double entendre or tautology? Season over, they stayed in their town club digs for longer than strictly needed, buying a big Mercedes to throw their squatters' hats in the back as they drove. Some would even catch a train to Sydney, there to take delivery of a Rolls-Royce. There being no machine or manual car wash places in those days, every Roller and Merc in town looked like hell come in from dusty western plain.

Truth be known the shearing contractor's truck looked better. It looked at home, in its natural habitat. It had spotlights on top, spare fuel cans on the side along with canvas waterbags cooling their contents off, a luggage rack full of swags on top ready for a kip at a moment's notice, two dogs standing guard, and a winch and ropes on the bull bar poking out front. Horses for courses, eh? Why would you bring a mudrunner out here? It was either bone dry or flooding, once in a while when la Niña was favourable. Even the shearing contractor and his gang took a brief sabbatical at such times.

The stationary Roller and Merc and tractor and truck and livestock had to survey the brown surrounding sea from higher ground, or see nothing from behind a levee bank. All manner of wildlife slipping, sliding, hopping, slithering, burrowing, swimming, crawling and emerging found themselves sharing the same space. Mosquitos left their many proboscis marks on exposed skin, and, as floodwater had receded just so, out came the stinging pinprick swarm of sandflies from the sandy border line of the Moola Moola River. Happy days when the heat and the dry and the dust chased those insect symphonies away.

Snail mail in those days was too snail for the lawyers. Finn, and the others, operated a legal courier system that guaranteed next day service to and from wherever. One day Finn frowned at an envelope that came through the post. He checked the postmark date as usual, and had his front office log the correspondence, file it, date it – both written and received – and put it on a timeline for action. Unusually, he also asked that the envelope be filed, which puzzled the staff somewhat. He did not elaborate, and they didn't ask.

He had checked that envelope as he rotated it. No return address. It was post-marked with yesterday's date. Post Office – Moola! A file was created and stored alphabetically under O for O'Hanlon J, number 1970/456, and recorded in the rolling logbook both by date received and the letter O. Finn asked that it be actioned immediately.

The years had successfully eroded most of Finnbar's soft County Kerry brogue, but not the phrases that came automatically into play. 'Well, if I was going to do this, I wouldn't be starting from here,' he mused, softly whistling a County Kerry air. Even so, he put the cash payment from the envelope, together with other cheques, into the day's banking satchel.

He could not have imagined the role he was to play in it. Not central by any means, but it could not have happened without him. His was a necessary but not sufficient condition. Blame Finn's propensity to be helpful wherever he could, and not just when cash reward was involved. Blame also his natural inclination to sniff out a good story. This one, he thought, had all the makings of a ripper. He determined to jolly it into life.

He was to ponder that envelope and the mystery it contained many times in the near future, as a strange story constructed around its contents.

Boat

'So long, *New York, howdy East Orange.*'

Bob Dylan

The Seamen's Union of Australia was very strong in the 1950s. Coastal shipping was reserved for union members only. Foreign ships could dock at one Australian port only and then be gone. Gradually automation, containerisation, and flags of convenience ships infiltrated this closed workplace, aided by the policies of Bob Menzies governments. That militant union, with strong left-wing inclinations, remains to this day, 2023, Maritime Union of Australia, but somewhat subdued.

Jen left Jindabyne in 1969 by bus along bumpy gravel roads, ticket to Bega. Except she got off at Cooma where the bus turned right for the south coast of New South Wales. One hundred kilometres further north, she took one night in the Civic Hotel in Canberra to recover. To this day, that city can't find its downtown, and relies on the name 'Civic' for such status. Two other centres – Tuggeranong and Woden – vie for attention, but steadfastly remain on the lower steps of the podium. Walter Burley Griffin, architect 'father' of Canberra, called it 'Civic Centre' on the elegant drawings done by his wife Marion Mahoney Griffin, and the name stuck, albeit one word only, a diminutive homage to big Walter. Marion was ignored by history.

Suitably refreshed, the soon-to-be minted Mary caught a bus

to nearby Queanbeyan, and then the train to Central Station, Sydney. She walked the way to People's Palace in Pitt Street. It provided affordable accommodation for single people and families. There she cut her hair, roughly, and bleached it a bit over the sink, using peroxide sparingly. She changed into different clothes, still dowdy, but was now a new person unrecognizable from the former. She threw her old clothes into a bin in the street.

She went to the cinema one night, a treat not available in Jindabyne, enchanted by the pianist that emerged from the stage floor and tickled the ivories before the screen lit up.

Martin Place then, as now, was Sydney's financial centre. Mary went into three banks, one after another, and purchased a bank draft in each. They were as good as cash, for any bearer could present them to any bank or business without question. Each was of a not overly suspicious size. The bundle of bank notes in her shoulder bag diminished somewhat.

She went into a succession of ritzy jewellers and pulled out a diamond or two. Each jeweller whistled in admiration through his squinting eyepiece. Mary showed them a copy of grandma's will, which fully described the jewels. She also showed a certificate of assessed value. Thus assured, they paid her the price she demanded, no offers accepted.

She was now ready to move further north. Newcastle was and is the world's largest coal port. In Hunter Street she went into three banks, one after the other, car dealers in between, for three more bank drafts. She took great care with her shoulder bag, never letting it out of sight. It looked so daggy that no self-respecting young woman would ever be seen dead in it.

That suited Jen just fine. No thief would eye it off for potential snatching. Together with her daggy 1950s clothes, Mary was no thief's mark. She could have fitted in alongside the occasional beggar in the street. The only difference was, she was clean and would always deposit a coin into the beggar's hand.

She walked into the Seamen's Union office in Newcastle West. Mary Chiaprisi paid her dues in cash. She was now a card bearer, union member, legit to work at sea. There were no questions asked. They enthusiastically gave her all the information necessary, made some phone calls, and typed her a letter. With that, she was to sign onto the *Mary Ganter*. Ship's cook. Experience? Eight years in shearer country. Good enough. New Mary had decided to float her chances on a rising tide.

She bought a cook's uniform, not strictly necessary except to herself. They sailed next morning on board her namesake. Mary is as Mary does. The crew said they had never tasted such perfectly cooked breakfasts, crispy bacon, eggs sunny side up, good coffee, such smiling service. She put up with the cramped cabin in steerage, and the long demanding hours. She was one of those landlubbers that did not suffer sea sickness. Some of the crew, old hands, did.

There was brief respite from the constant motion, as the *Mary Ganter* called into ports at Port Kembla, Eden, Melbourne, Geelong, Portland, Adelaide and finally after the longest and roughest leg of all, Fremantle. Phantom motion stayed with Mary as she sway-walked each waterfront for a day of the ship's loading and unloading. Smelly dockside navvies, Jackie Howes, hairy armpits, and bulging biceps did not bother Mary in the least. Martin had smelled much worse, a dishonest stink to boot. There was not enough time to go further than the nearest Port Café, always the same name, no matter what the port. That's where the whole crew ate, just for a change. Mary was happy with the seamen's company on those days off. They all reckoned that Mary's food was better. Why hadn't Martin ever praised her?

She signed off at Fremantle on docking one morning, before the 'Fremantle Doctor' had time to start blowing its worst. That wind did cool off scorching Perth each afternoon. Small boats on Swan Reach sought refuge for that while. Jennifer Spring-O'Hanlon thus vanished.

The Articled Clerk

Carmel Blount was part of a girls' clique at primary school in Jindabyne, known to all and sundry as Jindy. That growing hamlet did not have a high school. All kids had to be bussed to Cooma, where post-war migrant families lived by the thousands. Their menfolk worked on the Snowy Mountains scheme, Australia's biggest civil engineering construction ever. It generated hydro power and irrigation water by capture, diversion, and storage of snow melt from the high country. The east-flowing water became a dribble, and the west-flowing Murrumbidgee and Murray rivers transported the diverted Snowy River waters, only to be captured by more irrigation dams downstream. That's why old Jindabyne township was re-located in the 1960s, to the shores of a mighty new body of trout-filled water, Lake Jindabyne. It slowly became a fully fledged lakefront town behind Jindabyne Dam as it filled up over several years. Old Jindy drowned, leaving only its ghosts to hover.

Jindy kids like Eva, Tom, Jennifer, and Carmel were anything but country hicks by the time they had spent time at Cooma State High, a twenty-language babble at lunch recess. Carmel was a bright girl, and planned herself a future way beyond its time, for a girl that is. Law schools discouraged girls from enrolling. They obliged and didn't in droves. On two hands you could count the female lawyers in New South Wales at the time.

Carmel wasn't popular. She wasn't unpopular. She was studious, neither pretty nor ugly, just handsome in a way that takes time to reveal a beautiful woman. Ugly duckling is the term. Clever Carmel was dux of her class, debating champion, and she ran and swam faster than the boys. She wasn't a goody-two-shoes either. They thought she was a little humourless, that's all. She had outgrown toilet jokes before any other toddler. She had discovered *The Goon Show* on radio well before the others.

Trouble really was, by teenagerhood, those pop-song-loving contemporaries of Carmel's just weren't high enough in the brow to get her Beethoven jokes. She was cracking good fun if you could just get up to her level. For all that, she was no snob. Goons Peter Sellers, Spike Milligan, and Harry Secombe always made her laugh.

Carmel was one of those gifted children that would have prospered under any education system. She would have thrived under the tutelage of Cistercian monks, humble rural schools, home schooling, and of course in the best private schools in the land. She later proved herself with what came her way, or more to the point, with what she made come her way.

Her real gift was to perceive what she had missed out on, and then to make good on that deficit by self-education or seeking help once she got to university. She was never overwhelmed by her situation. She was mildly jealous of the education of the privileged class in Sydney, those who attended St Ignatius College Riverview.

Law school in Sydney was out. Not enough money to pay, not enough family connection to influence. Instead, after school she went straight to work with Harry Lasseter, front office. Frugal to a point, she saved like Scrooge McDuck. She worked second and third jobs for two years. Harry had never seen anything like it.

The third year saw her at Sydney University Law School, the only female there. The alumni of that bastion of privilege could do nothing to stop the onslaught of Carmel once they hit that level playground. She outshone all the others, including the judges' sons, forcing the powers that be to award her a scholarship. She, a gold medal honours graduate in five years.

Not for Carmel the usual path. She went to a country practice and emerged as Articled Clerk. Who was Finnbar Mahoney's sidekick when the receptionist handed him the envelope posted the day before in Boolaba? None other than Carmel Blount.

Hiding in Plain Sight

The hourly bus transported Mary Chiaprisi from Fremantle to the city. The cook's uniform went into a bin. On went her dowdy. She caught a cab to West Perth, to a real estate agent. It took her no time flat to organise inspections of suitable houses. That dragged on the whole leg-weary day. Tired and foot sore, she retreated to her cheap hotel.

Next day, she returned to the agent and asked for the contract for her chosen already vacant cottage. He was astonished, having taken her for a tyre kicker, a waste of space. He was even more astonished at her skill in negotiating the price down and down. She never mentioned horse trading which was far more shifty and risky. After all, a house couldn't die of colic next day.

She ordered the nearest conveyancing solicitor to advise on the contract immediately. Not accustomed to anyone making such a demand, let alone a mere female, he said to come back Friday. She said, 'Now or I'll find someone who will. It's only a standard contract after all. I can read it in five minutes. So can you. Take your lunch five minutes late!'

She paid for the all-clear typed out legal advice in cash. The secretary who did the typing did not complain. All she said was that no one had ever spoken to her boss like that and gotten away with it. Mary engaged her dimples and flashed her pearly whites. They outshone her dowdy dress.

How soon could she move in? As soon as the owner had been paid in full. She didn't even pay a deposit. Instead, she opened the fashion-blind bag from her lap and pulled out three of nine bank drafts. The real estate agent let out a slow whistle once his disbelief settled down. 'Can we go to a bank?'

They went to the nearby English, Scottish and Australian Bank, to pay the agreed sale price direct into the seller's account. That way she could avoid the hassle and delay of the Trust Account. The teller called for the manager. In those days, he – always a 'he' – was a pre-eminent citizen, and not to be off-sided if you wanted any financial future. Mary was ready for him.

'Why are you paying with bank drafts?'

'Because you won't let women have their own cheque books.'

Where did you get so much money from?'

'I didn't rob a bank, if that's what you are asking.'

'No no, I didn't mean that at all.'

'Then I don't know what you mean. Do you ask all men where the money came from?'

The manager was flummoxed, and his discomfiture showed. Of course not. Then of course not me neither. The manager asked his secretary to type out a receipt, and he signed it.

As if to appease the bank manager, she opened an account in the name of Mary Chiaprisi, naturally. In went another bank draft. It was September 1969. Ten years married to Martin, he now living solo back in Jindabyne.

Mary went back to the realtor's office. Keys please. That man had never completed a faster sale. Tyre kicker indeed! Mary went inside and surveyed her new kingdom. By that evening she had furnished it with hard-bargained second hand furniture, paid for in cash, receipted to Chiaprisi M. It was completely fashionable, rich folk cast-offs, in contrast to her own appearance. First things first – the dress shops of Subiaco would have to wait.

Next day she went to the Bank of New South Wales, West Perth

Branch, to open a bank account with another bank draft. In the name of Jennifer O'Hanlon, proofed by her Birth Certificate. The manager was called. You can't open a bank account without your husband's approval. Sir, did I ask you if you are married? No. Then don't ask me. But it's bank policy. And it's my policy not to tell you something that's none of your business. Then I can't open an account for you. She flashed a bank draft for five thousand dollars, a lot of money back then, and said I will take this to a bank that will. Money always talks, so he opened an account and gave her the passbook. And the cheque book? You need your husband's approval. I'm not married. Why didn't you say so earlier? Because it's none of your business. He issued her a cheque book.

The deflated manager hadn't wanted to face any more of her repartee and lose even more face. Within a week, she had wrangled the title deeds to her house from the Office of Titles. This was a valuable document for later proof of identity for when she went for a driver's licence. She carefully kept her New South Wales one, proving she was Jennifer O'Hanlon.

She now had bank accounts and cheque books under her new name. Good for proof of new identity. She had another under her old name. That would come in handy later. She did one transaction using that account – Jennifer O'Hanlon bought one thousand shares in Poseidon at eighty cents each. She had heard rumours about a nickel strike not yet made public. Insider trading was not illegal back then.

In those days, the only way to get cash was to cash a cheque at the bank. If you paid for bigger purchases by cheque, first you had to wait until the bank cleared the proceeds before you could collect whatever it was. Forged cheques were the forerunner to today's internet scams. Mary carefully complied. The ES&A manager always smiled at her on entry, and she never baited him again, or looked anything but sweet and undemanding. The manager knew otherwise, and navigated cautiously as she conducted her business. The manager never asked. It was none of his business. He knew he would be told. It became ANZ Bank a year later.

Marketing types had also won the day and condemned the name 'New South Wales' to the dustbin of history. The manager of the newly minted Westpac Bank never raised an eyebrow when in early 1970 she deposited $180,000, the proceeds of sales of one thousand Poseidon shares. Nor one or two more bank drafts later that year. He assumed that she came from a family of means. That she had, via grandma. She was self-made via Poseidon.

By now, she was Perth-girl authentic. One day the daily two weeks old Sydney Morning Herald paid her a dividend with this death notice: '*Louise Jackson, grand-daughter of Harry Lasseter, Solicitor, late of Jindabyne, wishes to announce his death on 11 May 1970. Aged 85. Died peacefully at home. Funeral at Jindabyne Cemetery 16 May. No flowers. Donations to the Salvation Army, Cooma*'.

Mary knew that now was the time for more to be done. At the end of May, she flew Trans Australia Airways to Adelaide – no more tramp steamers for her. It took her a few days to walk around the inner suburbs to admire the vintage stone houses created by German craftsmen well used to that building material. A reasonable amount of time had lapsed since Harry had died. Grabbing quill and vellum, she hand-wrote a request for legal work, signed it, put some bank notes in, licked a stamp, addressing the envelope:

Mahoney & Geeves, Solicitors

Moola Moola NEW SOUTH WALES.

She didn't know that firm from a bar of Burfords, having found it in a telephone directory at the Adelaide GPO in King William Street. She didn't know where Moola Moola was on a map. Then she put it into a bigger envelope, licked another stamp, looked up another random phone number:

Mrs W Britten

Emerald Street

Boolaba NEW SOUTH WALES

In Boolaba, who but who opened the envelope from someone unknown, no return address, and posted its contents onwards to Mahoney & Geeves, Moola? Eva Britten, née Eva Rumford, formerly of Jindabyne.

There's a Bridle Hanging on the Wall

As Mary ensconced herself in her new life, she planned her conversion to squirrel. Martin back in Jindy had his life planned for him, unwillingly, unfortunately. He hung his bridle on the wall. He eschewed riding boots for felt slippers. His tinnitus faded as spurs jangled no more. He settled into unhappy invalidity.

Then a curious crime happened. 1970. The sergeant was young and new and didn't instil confidence in the locals. His predecessor was old school and gnarly. Bob Paxton looked just out of school. His curly hair added a bunch of height to his inadequate stature, but nothing to his gravitas and projection of authority. Jindabyne folk were surprised, however, after they had shaken hands with him. He had a grip as fierce as a crab's claw. Then they changed tune just a little, conceding only that maybe he was not too weak to win but only maybe too strong to lose. Poor bugger Bob – how could he ever get on top? In that, the locals had underestimated his ability to evolve with the situation. He was ambition unbound.

Horse theft not in his ken. Horses didn't get stolen in Sydney where he came from. He studied the evidence and couldn't fathom quite how the horses ended up in the Cooma saleyard. The angry grazier owner found out a week too late. Why weren't they still back in the paddock where he had left them? Stock and station agents Elder Smith Goldsborough Mort were not happy. They had to bear the costs. Though they followed procedure, they had not spotted a deception.

The horses after a week could be goodness knows where, their brands long altered beyond recognition. How the hell do you put six horses up for auction behind the owner's back and he has no inkling? And all the paperwork looked legit! That is, if you didn't look too closely. Sergeant Bob Paxton sure as hell didn't know. Those papers looked genuine. They must have been forged though. But by whom? That was the two-thousand-dollar question, the value of those six. The exchange was completed by Elder Smith Goldsborough Mort Limited, selling agents, on consignment.

The horses had been delivered to their yards by Herb Benninger. He was known for his honesty, not a blemish to his name. Not even a person who could 'help police with their inquiries'.

The 'seller' was easily traced, a respectable local grazier that caught, bought, and sold horses, as did many a man on the land of 'The Man from Snowy River'. There was no shortage of brumbies in the mountains, hardy, genetically toughened by natural selection, and with legendary tenacity and endurance, even if a little ordinary in appearance.

Paxton scratched his head, and decided that a unique crime had been committed. It took him quite a time scouring the Cooma Court records when – bingo! Back in 1969 there was a similar case. So not unique, just unusual. Martin O'Hanlon had done time over the exact same scam.

What's more, locals told Paxton that Martin was still around, and where he lived, retired and secluded. The sergeant found Martin at home, barely able to shuffle his slippers around. He was helped to stay at home by people that did his shopping for him, cooking a week's supply for him, and phoning each day. Clearly, he was no repeat offender. If he ever was even a one-timer. Martin insisted he never was no criminal and that he was just the fall guy, an easy mark for the police prosecutor.

How did the horses get to the Cooma saleyards? Paxton checked that out, and soon was satisfied the barely literate bum-fluff boy Adam Yates could not have been the forger. Bumfluff still lived at home. Mum and dad said he left school because he had trouble learning to read and write. He too had been taken for a ride, and not on his usual station round-up horse that was his day job. He was driving Martin O'Hanlon's horse transporter. The horses first went to his place. Next day, Bumfluff drove them from Martin's to Cooma Saleyards.

Martin bristled. 'Check it out. The paperwork must still be on record. I never delivered the horses to the saleyard. My truck, yes, driven by Bumfluff. I was shown as the legitimate owner, yes, but no money ever went into my account. So how come I was guilty of fraud and horse theft? The cops pinned it on me because I was easy pickings. I was listed as the seller, no dispute. But I can tell you now, I was not *the* seller. That bastard is long gone. Like the six horses. Why don't you go looking for that ne'er do well Tom Dooley? I was sure he did it, but the bastard was always too sharp for me,' bitched Martin.

Paxton wondered how the hell did a copycat get hold of the original scam? Or was it the same crook? Paxton went looking for Tom Dooley. Was he up to his old tricks? Yes. His scams had spread as fast as rabbits before there was myxomatosis. On his way, Tom had bashed aside the right questions and walked past answers that might have set him straight. He never had a moment of moral encounter. It got too hot for him in Jindy as people figured him out. With his shifty habits he had nowhere safe to run to, but he ran just the same. How could he feel safe when he never tried to understand the risks? His thefts were not really enough to call in the cops, but enough for his victims to tell him to eff off when detected.

He was easily traced as he moved his petty life elsewhere. Trouble was, there was no permanent elsewhere for him. His efforts were charming, just too bad they came from a snake charmer. He quickly wore out his welcomes, in spite of his good looks and smooth words. The emphasis was on 'loose' that he somehow wore on his sleeve, right alongside 'heartless'. He was drawn to deeds of dangerous attraction, and never developed a sense of prudence. He moved often. He couldn't hold down a job for long before the boss found things a bit skew whiff where they weren't before. Piss off, Tom!

Tom never thought about covering his tracks. He would write letters home to tell his folks how well he was doing. Even they decided that their beloved handsome Tom Dooley was loose with the truth, but loved him just the same. Paxton's one phone call to them uncovered Tom at Dubbo, a big enough mid-western New South Wales town to accommodate him for quite a while.

The sergeant called on him there a week later. It soon became clear that Tom had done no recent horse scamming in Cooma. He had left a shitty little trail of his pettiness around Dubbo, easy to find but hard to prosecute because the victims were embarrassed to be so easily scammed. Besides, it was never for much. It would cost more to go to court than it was worth. Better to just warn their friends. It would take a fair while before most of Dubbo had been forewarned to tell handsome Tom to eff off.

Paxton then took Tom back to 1969 when Martin O'Hanlon was branded a horse thief and went down for six months. 'Had Tom set him up?'

'No way,' said Tom. 'I would have had to organise horse transport to the saleyards. I would have had somehow to steal those horses. How the hell could I have done that? Check with livestock carriers – there were only three of them around Jindy. They will tell you. Their delivery dockets will tell you. Somehow or other, I was a victim of this scam as much as poor Martin. He was set up because he was a man who could transport horses around the country. Cops wanted a conviction, so fabricated a case against him. And the poor bugger goes to gaol!'

Paxton believed Tom in spite of his shiftiness. The evidence against Martin O'Hanlon did not stand the pub test. It didn't pass, as far as the sergeant was concerned, the legal test either. As he talked around town about the rustling case in Cooma, all the locals said they had only believed Martin was guilty two years earlier because the law had found so.

As they scratched their heads over time, gradually they too realised that Martin was innocent, and took him back into the fold. By then the scandal had cost him his marriage, and Martin struggled on alone, not looking too healthy either as time went by. Poor bugger, Martin. They took it upon themselves to make sure that Martin was okay on his own. That was the least they could do, having let him down in his time of need. It looked as though the horse scammer had gotten away with it.

The Auctioneer

Bill Britten was two years ahead of Eva Rumford at Cooma High. BB King was already one of the most important names in rhythm and blues music in the 1950s. Naturally Bill was BB to all and sundry. He presented as meek, but not meek enough to inherit on Judgment Day. He had a quiet strong strength. Eva had a crush on him but never let on. They began sitting together on the Jindy school bus. It developed from there until they were inseparable. A few years later they were married.

BB took a job with Elder's, short for Elder Smith Goldsborough Mort Limited, a mouthful for casual talk. This dream job was trainee stock and station agent and auctioneer. Eva was happy to go wherever Bill went. A match made in heaven, you might say. His next posting in 1970 was to Boolaba, western New South Wales. Neither had ever heard of it. No matter. It came with a house and car.

It was a bit of a shock when they got there. A dry and dusty little place reliant on the wool industry. First thought – if Mother Earth ever needed an enema, this is where you'd insert the tube. It didn't matter to BB though. Here he would learn his trade. It was always going to be amid dust and flies. No sheep had ever drunk from the Pacific Ocean. It turned out he had plenty of sales to attend with his mentor – prize rams, sheep, some cattle, and the occasional property preceded by the usual auction of machinery and contents.

They could afford a car. They really had to afford that second hand Morris Minor. That was the only way that Eva could get to her job as a chalkie at the Moola Primary, twenty minutes away. It was a happy household in that Elders' house, that came fully furnished with the job.

Over the dinner table, Eva and Bill swapped the usual chit chat, sometimes reminiscences. A bit about work, not about clients, mind, for they knew the dangers of gossip in small towns. It was about births, weddings, footy in a minor way because they had to be able to engage the locals if asked about the weekend match, the weather, holidays, funerals, all that sort of stuff. That was to change when Finnbar Mahoney asked to have a chat. They had never met him and looked up the phone directory to learn that he was a lawyer.

The Plight of the Unicorn

'There was green alligators, and long-necked geese,

Some humpty-backed camels and some chimpanzees,

Some cats and rats and elephants, but sure as you're born,

The loveliest of all was the unicorn.'

Shel Silverstein

Carmel Blount had a strictly work relationship with Mahoney &
Geeves. One day that changed just a tad. She had been working
there for a few years. After work, Finn invited her to his club for
a 'social chat' that was really to do with work, but he wanted to
keep it just between the two of them.

Women were not accepted as members. Women could not enter
alone. Women had to be admitted by a member. They had to
leave when their 'signatory guardian' left. That's how Carmel
described it to Finn when the process came known to her – to her
surprise and no little offence, one might add. She was a feminist
original, ahead of her time. His opening gambit, for such it was,
caught her totally offside.

'You never socialise about town. It's not my business, but for
quite a while now each month I give you Friday off after twelve
and then Monday before twelve. You catch the train to Sydney,
and that's just fine by me. Would I be expecting a wedding
invitation then?'

The twinkle in his eye took away any offence. Carmel was near speechless, stuttering, 'No! What a thing to ask!'

'Sorry, it's none of my business, but what do you do?'

Finnbar softly whistled a bar of 'Danny Boy' when she said, 'I spend two days in the Law School Library. I'm writing my PhD thesis.'

An awkward silence settled at that coffee table, between mentor and mentee. Carmel's brow did a little furrow, a prelude familiar to Finn. Carmel automatically read the relief of his mind, and the pair burst out laughing. That particular ice was broken, or rather melted and evaporated, such was the feeling of levity that followed.

More 'Danny Boy'. 'Holy Mother of Jesus! I always knew you were way smarter than me. Now this! You! Carmel, you must be wondering why I'm discussing work away from work. It must seem strange. Let me explain. It's just between the two of us.'

Finn told her about the written request to finalise a name change by deed poll, just a procedural thing. The form has been completed and duly notarised by a practising solicitor. 'It's all above board. I've already done it and lodged it. The firm of solicitors that originally did the work doesn't exist in New South Wales. Mary Flamboya now exists legally. Trouble is, we have no idea who she was or where she is.'

Clever Carmel, 'You will know by the forwarding address.'

Finn acknowledged with, 'Logical Carmel. But the forwarding address is c/o Poste Restante, Alice Springs, Northern Territory. All I know is that the request to register the name change was originally posted in Adelaide, no return address. The strange part is, it was not addressed to me.'

Carmel puzzled, 'Then how did it get to you?'

'It was sent by someone in Boolaba, according to the postmark. Without a return address we don't know who. Can you help me find out without anybody else knowing? This sender wants to really remain hidden, and I want to know why. There's a mystery to be solved, and I want you and I to solve it. Up for it?'

Carmel knew that you could change your name by deed poll in total confidence, and then disappear from your abusive husband or whatever. This was an entirely different level – a disappearance, legal footwork done by a now non-existent practice. Who was the person that requested its registration? Who in Alice Springs was going to pick it up?

'I'll ring the postmaster at Boolaba in the morning. They have very little mail, and he's sure to remember who sent it a few days ago.'

'Great stuff. When you find out, let me know. We'll just sit on it. I get a feeling that nothing that will help us will be happening for a while.'

Carmel could see that too. A phone call next day gave the answer. Carmel added Mrs W Britten's name to the unofficial file that only she and Finn ever saw. Mrs Britten, non-plussed by that request, retrieved another envelope from her wicker wastepaper basket under her desk. She dropped it at Finnbar's front office next day. It seemed so utterly benign.

A month or two went by and Carmel's PhD thesis was complete by the time Finn re-ignited their detective work. Carmel was starting to think about a boyfriend. That would have to wait until she moved to Sydney to join a prominent judge. And that would happen only after she knew who was Mary Flamboya.

They met after work at the club, and sat down deep in the dark leather big-armed brown lounge chairs, the colour of big-armed shearers. The hovering waiter brought them drinks to side tables. 'Carmel, what do you tink we can do next to find our mystery lady?'

Carmel smiled at the pronunciation and laid it on a bit thick in her reply, 'I *think* two *things*. She has waited for the dust to settle before she took the legal step. That means she thinks that nobody has any interest in her anymore. Water under the bridge and all that. The second thing is that she now feels safe to use that name officially. What could that be for? Well, I reckon someone as smart as mystery Mary would want to start running a business. She could have run a café or hairdresser in any name at all. No, she is registering a company, and needs to be legally recognised to become a company director. We need to do a company search, and find that director.'

Finn paid no heed to her teasing. 'Great tinking, Carmel. I tink the same. We're going to find us a unicorn.'

'But the unicorn does not exist.'

'That's why we have to find one! Let's you and I start by having a chat with Mr and Mrs W Britten. Better you phone them, Carmel. I can sometimes gab too much, the Irish in me you know.'

Carmel just stroked her handsome intelligence and said, 'I'm with you.'

Eva and Bill chatted that evening, mystified by an invitation to meet with a couple of solicitors at the Moola Club. They decided it was an example of country town friendliness, and networking. Besides, they had never set foot inside that inner sanctum of male superiority.

At the door, Finn enthused with Irish informality, 'Eva and Bill, it's yourselves then!' They introduced each other, Finn signed them in, and they sat down deep in brown leather. The waiter with bow tie hovered. Eva looked at Carmel in faint recognition. BB did the same. 'Haven't we met before?' queried Eva.

Carmel, mind like a trap, said, 'We used to be on the school bus to Cooma, Bill too. I never knew you and BB were an item. And I honestly had no idea that you were way out here. Fancy that.'

Smiles all around with genuine pleasure. Finn's mind was working overtime. Smart Carmel's didn't need overtime. She went straight into action on a seemingly innocent line of inquiry. Eva was nobody's fool either, and was not fooled by Carmel's question, 'Do you keep in touch with anybody from Jindy?'

'Carmel, I had no idea you were in Moola. Last I heard was that you were in Law School. Then BB and I married and after a couple of years moved to Boolaba, and started the rest of our lives. You are here about the letter I dropped in to Mahoney & Geeves, aren't you? You must know who it came from as soon as you opened it, surely?'

'Well, no,' said Carmel calmly, hiding her discomfiture at having been found to be so obvious. She was not used to that. 'Do you have any idea?'

Eva and BB had no idea either. Finn sidled and insinuated his conversation in sideways, and gradually the evening turned out to be just another friendly social. Carmel read Finn like a book and kept the talk to town small talk. This time Eva did not get their drift, not that it really mattered.

In Finn's mind, Eva had already started to solve the mystery for them without even knowing it. Everybody enjoyed the evening, Carmel and Finn included. They said we must do this again soon. Eva and BB agreed. It was such a change from Boolaba with its one pub and bowling club.

Next day at work, Carmel asked where to now? Finn said that he wanted the names of all her friends in her year on the Cooma run, the year they were born, moved, married, spouse name and so on. Finn called it his unicorn finder. Carmel handed him a short list next day. She knew not to delay. Finn was on a roll. This is what she wrote:

NAME	BORN	MOVED	MARRIED	SPOUSE	BORN
Carmel	1939	Sydney 1960	No		
Tom	1939	Lots	Not in her time		
Martin	1918	Cooma 1969	1959	Jen Spring	1938
Eva	1938	Boolaba 1970	1965	Bill Britten	1936
Jennifer	1938	Bega? 1969	1959	O'Hanlon	1918

Finn wrestled. 'It's a start, Carmel. Still doesn't get us far. The only query I have is Jennifer Spring. She moved to her aunt in Bega.'

'Yes, she had an aunt there and used to go there for holidays a couple of times a year. I was already long gone and lost touch with schoolmates. Jen married the year I left. I could not go to the wedding. Too busy, you know.'

'Why did Martin move to Cooma?'

'Well, he didn't really move, he was taken.'

'Who's talking Irish now? What do you mean?'

'He got six months for horse theft, minus two for good behaviour. He was back home after four months.'

Finn had a practice to run. Carmel, he knew, was destined for greater things than articled clerk to a country solicitor. He was sad to see her go, said so, gave her his blessings, and wished her well. She carried her newly minted PhD with her to the judge's chambers where she began her rise to fame. Judge's associate.

The unicorn would just have to wait. Finn knew that unicorns do not just go away – they never have.

Dance the Tarantella

"'Dance, then where-ever you may be
I am the lord of the dance" said he'
Sydney Carter

Mary Chiaprisi danced the tarantella, danced it any time, and in dancing it she looked as good as anyone. Quite as though her life depended on it. In one way it did. It was her passport to this new existence, celebrating Italian festivals. She adopted their ways by osmosis. She could have been just someone who had migrated as a kid and had either forgotten the language or had never learned. Lots of migrant parents thought that speaking English at home was the right thing to do. Mary never explained herself to anyone. Why should she?

She knew that life could go on this way indefinitely. She had received marriage proposals. She was non-committal. Her suitors were understandably confused. She could not explain, other than to say, 'One day.'

The squirrel is industrious and stores nuts for the winter. The cricket just chirps. Mary felt as though she was that cricket. She should set about storing nuts for winter. At heart she was a squirrel. She did not want to perish next winter. She was as tough as a wombat's bum, and loved that a group of wombats was called a 'wisdom', probably dreamed up by some alliterative academic. Gaggle of geese anyone? Mary exhibited that tribal wisdom at every turn, always setting her personal compass to true north.

She did a quick re-run of the last couple of years. It was a way of stress-testing her situation. Was there any change of course that had to be made? By what clues could she be traced? Had she made a clean sweep of Jennifer Spring-O'Hanlon? What flowed from Martin's death and her suspicious looking disappearance? Once she came out of hiding, or worse, if the police discovered her whereabouts, how would she explain herself? Only questions. No answers. Thorough Mary made the following risk assessment check list:

Visit to Harry Lasseter – lips zipped.

Lasseter & Co – see 1.

L & Co receptionist – So what? Consultation no secret.

Bus to Bega – No secret. Got off at Cooma – who'd guess?

Bus driver – weak point for sure.

Civic Hotel Canberra – who'd remember? Who'd think to look there?

Sydney jewellers – saw only Grandma's will.

Sydney banks – cash transactions only.

Seamen's Union Newcastle – no worries.

Ship's master – ditto.

East Perth realtor, conveyancer, bank – low risk unavoidable.

School friends – hardly likely to throw much light on her flight.

Adelaide letter to Boolaba – low risk inevitable.

Letter to Moola – see 13.

Mahoney & Geeves – her mystery, theirs to solve.

Mary slept on that list and re-read it in the morning. She knew she couldn't undo any of it. 1971 gone long enough to be forgotten. Maybe. She had been biding her time.

'*The moving finger writes; and, having writ, moves on*'

The Rubaiyat of Omar Khayyam

She was pondering what her next move might be. Assessed the risk. Then she bought a Trans Australia Airlines ticket to Adelaide. Once she got there, a day later she bought an Australian National Airlines ticket to Alice Springs. One way only. There she waited for Poste Restante to conjure her a letter. It duly did a week later. That wait seemed interminable.

What if Mahoney & Geeves did not perform? What if it went to the bottom of the in tray? Why should that firm care? What if, what if, what if. That mid-summer week in the Alice was no picnic. At midnight, the mercury could still hover in the 40s C. Luckily there was no humidity, none whatsoever. Unluckily there was no air conditioner at that time. She just endured.

Bingo! Mary triumphed as she clutched that Mahoney & Geeves envelope, took out the 'Certificate of Change of Name by Deed Poll' and ripped the envelope to pieces into the hotel bin. Mary Flamboya wouldn't miss that shared toilet and bathroom down the corridor, nor the drunken hubbub that wafted up between the floorboards each night.

She did not fraternise with anyone. She paid up and went to the railway station. She bought a ticket to Port Augusta, on that swaying rocking narrow gauge train that took over a day to travel that near one-thousand-kilometre hell of a journey. She doze-dreamed of the luxury of that hotel in the Alice. Everything in life is relative.

Port Augusta didn't deserve a stop-over, but Mary had to recover somehow. A couple of nights there took her mind back to Alice Springs nights. Then a bus trip on rough roads every bit as hellish as the train returned her to Adelaide, and R&R in first class digs at the South Australian Hotel in North Terrace. TAA returned her to Perth as newly minted legal Mary Flamboya.

Death in Paradise

For a decade now, 2023, television crimes far more serious than horse rustling are being solved on an imaginary Caribbean Island called Sainte Marie. The London Metropolitan Police Service sends intrepid English and Irish detective inspectors, who never fail to solve impossible murders. Local female detective sergeants lend glamour and colour and social context. The interplay between them generates humour. *Death in Paradise* is not a serious business. More a sly spoof.

And yet, deadpan oddballs imported from London always solve each impossible case, get their man, sometimes their woman, sometimes more than one. Eccentric DI Humphrey Goodman is one such. His sidekick Detective Sergeant Florence Cassell compensates for his bumbling ways, and the murderers always end up behind bars.

Now just for the sake of fun, let your hair down and let's imagine that our 1970 Jindabyne Sergeant Bob Paxton had access to all those episodes to be aired some fifty years in his future. Imagine he watched them over and over. He figured that the repeats would hone his detective skills – how else in that backwater cop shop? It led him to a particular line of thinking. Had the law been properly enforced back in 1969 Jindabyne, Martin would never have ended up behind bars. Not guilty. He might have kept his wife. Now that's a bit doubtful, because in Sainte Marie many a marriage fails on the watches of the imported detective inspectors and detective sergeants. They aren't marriage counsellors. That's the way life is. In any event, when a marriage fails, does anyone blame the counsellor?

Just for fun though, thought Paxton, 'What could those super detectives in the Caribbean teach me here in little old Jindabyne? More to the point, what exacctly could I learn from any one Sainte Marie episode?'

Let's say Paxton picks a random episode – the thirty-sixth – and watches it a yet again. He puts up a corkboard in the station (whiteboards hadn't been invented). He writes up all he knows about the horse theft crime and sticks it up. That leaves a lot of space on the board. He'd add to it bit by bit. He also writes out a summary of the Sainte Marie murder story line on butcher's paper.

A sergeant's friend dies of heart attack.

He is grossly obese and in bad health.

He was dead man walking, for years.

The sergeant receives an impossible text on his phone.

It is from his dead friend.

Dead friend sent it to him during the delivery of his funeral speech!

Dead friend reveals that he has been murdered!

Why did bumbling Humphrey treat it as murder? That's the question Paxton asks himself. He makes a second list on butcher's paper.

Humphrey is a stickler, looks at every tiny detail.

The impossible text from the dead is a detail.

He goes over the death scene again.

Why has a pillow alongside the body got spittle on it?

Spittle should only have run down the victim's face.

Only the pillow under his head should show spittle, if any.

He orders a postmortem. It shows he was smothered.

The scam of 1969, Paxton distilled thus:

Horses taken to sale yards	Wed 5 March 1969.
Auction	Thurs 13 March 1969.
Horses discovered missing	Mon 17 March 1969.
Transport requested by	Tom Dooley.
Horse carrier	Martin O'Hanlon, driver Bumfluff.
Horses agisted at	Moonbah, Barry Way.
Form signed by	Rough initials only.
Horse descriptions	Detailed, including brands.
Location of Saleyards	Saleyards Road Cooma.

Bob scratched his head and puzzled whether Tom was really involved, other than to have his name 'borrowed' by the perpetrator. Bob also found out by talking around town that it was not unusual to have horses sold without written contract. Local trust and all that.

He distilled the scam of 1970 thus:

Horses taken to sale yards	Wed 11 March 1970.
Auction	Thurs 12 March 1970.
Horses discovered missing	Mon 17 March 1970.
Transport requested by	Jack Halvorsen.
Horse carrier	Herb Benninger.
Horses located at	Tarrangower, Snowy River Way.
Form signed by	Rough initials only.
Horse descriptions	Detailed, including brands.
Location of saleyards	Saleyards Road Cooma.

Paxton scratched his head. Again and then some more. What doesn't add up? Nothing on the face of it. Bumfluff boy Adam Yates was the horse transporter driver, not Herb Benninger. Why that deception? Why him and not Herbie? Clearly a clever conman had invented a new horse theft con. An innocent man had gone to gaol because the police were not clever enough. Now Jindy police were not the only ones, Bob told himself. Even in Sainte Marie some police jumped to premature conclusions, detective inspectors included, sometimes even the Commissioner of Police.

The paperwork for the auction of horses had been accepted as authentic by the stock and station agent. But then they did sometimes sell horses without contract at all, provided that the seller was someone well known to them. No surprise then that they didn't scrutinise the paperwork too closely. Usually it went straight to file, just for the record, just in case. Of what? Hardly ever tested.

This particular crime was only uncovered after the true owner discovered six horses missing. There could be quite a bit of time in between. Brumbies are after all perfectly happy in their own herds, free of human interference, for weeks on end. The Snowy Mountain mobs thrive human-unaided, generation after generation, period. No pampered racing nag would ever keep up with them on their mountain home, doped or otherwise.

The police would never have uncovered the crime by themselves, having no clue about the modus operandi of the conman. It took the aggrieved owner to do that. They were disinclined to believe him even then, until forced by the rather suspect paperwork once it had been finally thoroughly scrutinised. Then they displayed their true colours – a conviction, any conviction, was their measure of success. Many a dodgy policeman has planted evidence just to get another notch on his belt.

Bad luck for the cops that Martin had done time due to bad police work this time. They would be made to pay for that later, when that unsound conviction hit the headlines and public opinion made the police beat a hasty red-faced retreat. With the benefit of Paxton's hindsight, their sloppy work was a chronicle of scandal foretold.

The sergeant made a summary of the things he should be looking for. He mentally adopted DI Humphrey Goodman's Sainte Marie mode of thinking.

Sales dates.

Stolen horses straight taken far away.

First scam in Jindy 1969 Thursday 13 March.

Second in Cooma 1970 Thursday 13 March. Or should that be 12 March?

Forms must be forged.

Significance of names used.

Where were the horses' paddocks – near houses?

Bob scanned his list, furrowed his brow, stroked his chin, and his eyes suddenly widened momentarily. 'My! Sergeant Paxton, you must have had your eyes tested this week!' Dusk crept in on tiptoe. All was quiet save the whisper of the wind come home to roost. The wise old barn owl took flight. Fieldmice beware.

For the first time in his leapling life, Bob Paxton thought, 'What good luck to be born on 29 February!'

The Entrepreneur

'What's-a matter you? Hey! Gotta no respect Hey?

What-a you t'ink you do? Hey!

Why you look-a so sad? Hey!

It's-a not so bad. Hey!

It's-a nice-a place

Ah shaddap-a you face!'

Joe Dolce

Gen Z takes 2023 life for granted. Covid19 has forced a reassessment, but one should remember that in our time we all took the lifestyle of our time for granted. So did our parents. It's only when your accumulated years permit you before and after comparisons that you realise what it is that you have got that once you did not.

The octogenarian knows what it's like to feel 80, and what at twenty. The twenty-year old knows the now, but no idea about that 80 feeling. It is the fundamental law of life. You can bet that Aristotle's dad in 360 BC bitched about him sometimes. Why should today's youth be any different?

And so it is that the favourite caffè goes down without a second gen Z thought. Boomers, on the other hand, bless that bounteous gift. They couldn't get coffee like this when they were young.

Gen Zedders have their favourites, baristas that is. Why, there are even world championships! A boomer barista – what's that?

Mary Chiaprisi was a coffee aficionado well before the Aussie run-of-the-mill tea drinker converted to caffeine. The Italo-Australian Club of West Perth in 1969 had had an espresso machine from Milan when Mary first went there. It was already ten years old and looked like it.

That Jindy gal was smitten by the aroma, the texture, the viscosity that reflected just the right temperature of the milk froth added last by that steaming stainless pipe with a dog leg at the bottom bent toward the barista. The flourish that that young Italian hot blood operator gave at the end was the ultimate in style for country conservative Mary.

Small town Perth of the sixties was still British to its core, but with lively migrants now ensconced in their ghettos, doing what they always did back then before war tore their homes apart. The Brits brought everything bar their bowler hats with them, took their accents to tea houses for their non-alcoholic drink, and to bathroom-tile clad pubs for the mind-altering stuff. Civilized one minute, drunk the next.

What Mary liked was that the Italians sipped wine often but in moderation, making sure the vino spoke to the meal, and the dolce to the dessert wine. They didn't need booze to get started. If anything, Mary thought that sometimes they could do with tranquillizers to calm them just a tad when she couldn't tell if they were having a verbal or what? After a while, she wouldn't have it any other way.

Mary needed an outlet for her energy, and what's more, an outlet that made her money. She had quite a bit of capital, thank you Grandma's diamonds, thank you Poseidon. She had a stock of Italian friends, most of them prospering in their own businesses. For them, becoming a public servant was not an option. Their each English word ended in a vowel, if preceded by a consonant.

Sometimes an extra vowel was added to a vowel. A kind of language policy aimed at treating vowels kindly. That vowel was halfway between an e and an a. 'I tink-a it's-a time-a I leave-a.'

She never mimicked them. For her it was a charming way to talk. Sometimes she slipped into the same mode herself, hands and fingers frolicking in tune. Sometimes she couldn't shake a chorus out of her head.

She did a bit of market research. Not so many babies to come. The 1960s counterculture and the pill saw to that. Future people would come ready formed, ready trained, teeth straightened, appendices removed, ready to fill the labour shortages. Migration. The white Australia policy was in rigor mortis. Southern Europeans were welcome. Brits too of course, but with no advantage over Italians and Greeks who arrived in droves. Mary decided to surf the facts.

She went to Melbourne, to an accountant, who sold her an off-the-shelf company, the cheapest way. He read her out some names. She didn't like any of them. Thus Mary Chiaprisi became director of Forza Limited. Mary showed her bank account and house title deed as proof. No worries.

Back in Perth, Jim Driver CPA became company secretary. Mary Chiaprisi was the major shareholder, and Guiseppe (Joe) Martinelli the minor one. Then she went to a chartered accountant. He registered a holding company. A bit unusual, but he didn't raise an eyebrow that the deed poll legal Mary Flamboya was to be the sole owner. Tracing its activities could be done, but with difficulty. It would cost, and why would you? Time would tell.

Mary made sure to hide her legal deed poll name in a safe place, that is, in her safe. It should never see the light of day until absolutely necessary. That day was to come sooner than she thought. She went to her lawyer and made out her last will and testament. She herself typed a detailed folder of where all her important papers could be found, and who was her lawyer, accountant, banker and bank account numbers, next of kin, who to notify, and half the combination to her safe. The other half she left with her lawyer. She put her will in the safe, but the information folder in a place where it could easily be found.

She had letterhead paper printed, ditto company envelopes, and two business cards. Phone numbers by then were eight digits long, and WA had the prefix 08.

MARY CHIAPRISI	JOE MARTINELLI
DIRECTOR	SALES MANAGER
FORZA COFFEE	FORZA COFFEE
PH: (08) XXXX 0648	PH: (08) YYYY 0649

Mary set up a small office in West Perth, fitted out by Italian contractors, had the Postmaster-General's Department install two lines, plus a business touch dial phone with extensions on a reception desk. She had chosen her sales manager and minority shareholder Giuseppe Martinelli carefully, as was her wont. He had lived in Milan before Mussolini spoiled all that. War over, Joe migrated to Perth with his parents and started a landscape business – it didn't need perfect English. His business acumen and hard work saw it thrive in fast-growing Perth. He wasn't on the tools for long. He left that to his mainly Italian workforce.

He was just the right mature to give gravitas to the fledgling coffee enterprise. Mary knew what she did not have. She recognised what Joe did have. He knew Milan and its ways from ten years earlier. Taking a risk – Mary always took risks – she dispatched Joe to Italy. She wanted Forza to represent several companies – Faema in Milan, Lavazza in Turin, and Illy Caffè in Trieste. Her competition in Australia was Vittoria coffee, Sydney.

She was going to service the west, so far away from the east coast that some there still regarded it as a separate country. That it would have been if WA hadn't voted the way they did in 1900.

Mary, like many sandgropers, had an innate dislike of 'over east' in spite of herself being an easterner born and raised. She was confident that caffeine customers in WA would prefer local. She was going to give it to them.

Joe came back with exclusive agencies for Faema, Lavazza and Illy for the WA territory. She had no interest in the east. The first shipment of machines arrived not so long after. Joe hit the road and proved to be a salesman supreme. Forza not only supplied coffee machines and coffee but helped new entrepreneurs to set up cafes and coffee shops, based on models back in Italy. It was a kind of franchise without the heavy hand so beloved of other franchisors. Italian shopfitters were on hand.

Mary stayed in the background, until she judged the time was ripe. Under her impulsion, all charm, all smiles and all dimple, her great after-sales service became the signature of Forza Coffee. But she got herself a passport, Mary Chiaprisi, for future use. It was so easy in those days. You didn't have to jump through too many hoops back then – you just walked in and applied for one. Just in case they asked she had bank account and house deeds and birth certificate and driver's licence as proof. They did not ask.

She banked a weekly wage to Mary Chiaprisi, and another to Joe Martinelli. Jim Driver CPA whistled in admiration at their first profits. Joe Martinelli, macho Italian he, couldn't be prouder of Mary, the dividend he received, plus a generous bonus. More than any landscaper could ever earn. Mary paid herself a director's remuneration.

The West Perth Club had never seen two better dancers of the Tarantella than that evening. Their footwork would have put to shame Riverdance, that Irish show still years hence. Mary's clunky costume jewellery hanging around her ears and thereabouts, orbited her long red medieval dress with puffy sleeves and the odd stripe down.

'Slow down, you move too fast
You got to make the morning last'
Simon & Garfunkel

Dark Clouds in Jindabyne

Paxton had had just eight birthdays before his Jindabyne posting. 1970. He used to cry three years in a row because his siblings teased, 'Ha ha, you don't have a birthday, you don't have a birthday.' When 29 February finally came in the fourth year at his age four, Bob didn't get it. Why did big brothers not tease this year? He couldn't read that calendar by the fridge that had a red cross on the 29.

Now at the station, he thanked his lucky stars for having been born under a 29. He knew that a leapling's birthday fell on a different day each four years: 1964 Saturday, 1968 Thursday. He went back to his summary tables. Auction 1969 Thursday 13 March. Auction 1970 Thursday 11 March.

With his leapling's hat on, he doubled checked what he had written. Then came his ahaa! moment. The paperwork date of March 13 in 1970 was a Friday! Scammer's mistake. Sales were always held on the second Thursday of each month. The paperwork date should have been March 11. That meant only one thing – the scammer had to be a local! How else would he know that auctions were monthly second Thursdays in Cooma? He (presumably) was smart in one way and not so smart in another. Aren't we all? He had said Thursday knowing that was auction day. He had been careless with his paperwork. Who cares about the date? 'Sergeant Bob Paxton, that's who,' triumphed Sergeant Bob Paxton to himself.

In April he gathered half a dozen locals who might be implicated.

Or might help. Now, this wasn't strict police protocol – he should be interviewing suspects separately and comparing discrepancies in answers. He excused himself by telling himself that in Sainte Marie they sometimes interviewed a couple of possible witnesses at the same time, in order to conclude were they suspects or not. His list, he rationalised, comprised persons of interest assisting police with their inquiries, not yet suspects.

Bob wasn't pointing the finger at suspects when he met with Martin O'Hanlon and Bumfluff Adam Yates and Herb Benninger together. He was trying to unearth them. He moved on to interview the auctioneer from Elder's. He called in Tom Dooley from Dubbo. That didn't bother Tom – he was leaving town yet again, next stop Mudgee.

The chit chat went to and fro, side to side, front and back. At least twenty names were discussed and discarded. This was unusual police work to say the least. Bob agreed with their discardation. They included Harry Lasseter, long-time town solicitor who knew everything, told nothing. Each discard lacked at least one of means, motive, and opportunity. Bob was near giving up, and carelessly said to Martin, 'What about Jennifer O'Hanlon?'

Martin was mortified. He had never discussed his failed marriage with anyone, and he wasn't going to start now. Bob quickly said we have no interest in her. He knew he had trodden on a soft spot. He wasn't going to step on it again. He could instantly sniff the scent of a trail to be followed. He didn't want to give away a whiff of it.

Over the next week, he casually chatted with other women who had been Jen's classmates, and who had been dismissed as persons of even vaguely distant interest. Bob's concern now was in hearing the detail of Jen's marriage and her disappearance. Quickly he learned that Martin had been the original husband from hell. Poor Jen had been a virtual slave. She could not keep in touch with former girlfriends. She was seen only when she was running errands or doing the shopping. She was always anxious to get home. Martin was timing her absence from the bottom 40 – acres, that is – where he exercised horses for his clientele.

Enough said. Bob put on his law enforcer's thinking and took more soundings of his mind. His sympathy for the poor unfortunate Jen must not get in the way of his investigation. She had motive – Martin's machismo had provoked her, that's for sure. Nor were means and opportunity beyond her.

Bob decided she had to be it. Not guilty, mind, presumed innocent as the law requires, but the one most likely to do something out of revenge. He made an appointment to consult Harry Lasseter for 'legal advice'. He was going to commission his will. His real intention was to talk about another one. That's how they did it in Sainte Marie.

That night Bob celebrated a bit too much, starting at the pub and continuing in his police house home. Next morning, he had to shave the fur of his tongue with his toothbrush, and put a bit more than usual salt on his bacon and eggs. Oh, and a hefty dollop of Rosella Tomato Sauce.

Where There's a Will There's a Way

In his time, Bob Paxton had watched a lot of television – too much if you asked his mum. The usual stuff as a kid, going up the scale when his parents reckoned that he was ready. From them he caught the bug for drama. From them he sided with the British stuff, and reflected his parents' low opinion of the American. Nothing happens without a past, and Bob could not shake his. As a cadet policeman, crime drama captured his attention, and never left. He reckoned it was a good fit with his future career.

Bob watched repeated episodes of the crime dramas that were on offer in the 60s. So many times had the investigating detective inspector requested the relevant will. Always a will, a looking glass into motive.

He knew that to not be mentioned in a will was just as provoking as someone being in a will. If someone undeserving were in, someone who was out would get weaving, so to speak. Family members are entitled to get hold of a copy. They get hold of a copy. If out, that family member starts throwing shit in the fan. Sometimes murder. Greed greed greed.

They would go to a solicitor. They would look for forgery. They would look for multiple staple holes which might indicate later insertion of a page. They would look at page numbers. They would inspect each page foot for correct initials by all parties. One missing could give grounds for challenge. They would compare initials with full signatures at the signature page at the end. At the tiniest discrepancy, they would throw more shit at the fan. And really the only reason why was that they were not a beneficiary. They would conspire with similarly non-beneficiary sibling and cousin.

Martin O'Hanlon died in April 1970. He had looked like death warmed up for quite a while by then. He had ridden a horse only in his dreams for quite a while. The doctor wouldn't sign the death certificate without a postmortem. Now that was a bit unusual. He told Sergeant Bob Paxton what was going on. He said that, in his opinion, Martin showed classic signs of progressive strychnine poisoning.

Jeees, thought Bob. *First horse theft, next murder! And all on his first time in charge of a station!*

Bob went to Harry Lasseter soon after, in May 1970. Before getting down to specifics, he went out of his way to engage in small talk. How he was the new plod in town, how he found a welcome among the usual suspects (his chatty pun intended), and how others warily checked out their new not-to-be-messed-with.

He made sure to expand on his first challenge – horse rustling that happened as though the perpetrator were throwing down the gauntlet. Could Harry throw any light on that? No. Only then did Bob reveal something to Harry that was at this stage strictly between them. 'I have many a secret locked up here,' said Harry, tapping his forehead, which shook his eyebrows and made his lip whiskers twitch.

'It looks as if Martin O'Hanlon has been murdered! Detectives from Sydney will be on the case soon. In the meantime, I have to assemble all that I know. That's not a lot because I have been here for only six months. That slow poisoning must have been going on for years. Now, could I have a copy of Martin's will? Here is the necessary warrant.' He walked out with the will in a Lasseter & Co envelope. He read it before locking it in the safe.

Harry Lasseter died soon after, in May. The doctor signed the death certificate without demur. Harry was, after all, in his 80s. A life well-lived, a man much loved.

Martin's postmortem results came back shortly after Lasseter's demise. There was no doubt about. He had died of progressive strychnine poisoning, slowly accumulated in non-lethal doses.

A joint funeral was to be held, the biggest ever seen in Jindabyne, attended by foot soldier and burgher. Even former delinquents would turn up, grateful for Harry's part in their now straight and narrow. Martin was nowhere near the well-loved that Harry had been.

Two Sydney homicide detectives hit town soon after the surprise of the postmortem. The town was awash with rumour after the local rag broke the story. A whodunnit in Jindy! Whodathought! Where was the culprit? Was there a murderer in their midst? Or was somebody getting square from long ago and now far gone?

Bob set up an investigation room in the police station, corkboard and all, just like on the television. Bob kept it under lock and key except when investigators were in there. The corkboard had photos of those who had had dealings with Martin and his wife Jenny O'Hanlon née Spring. Tom Dooley, Carmel Blount, Adam Yates, Eva Britten née Rumford, William Britten, Harry Lasseter, Herb Benninger, auctioneers from Elder Smith Goldsborough Mort. Lots of others were considered but easily eliminated. The room also held two sheets of butcher's paper.

The conflab between the two Sydney detectives and Bob always led to one person of interest. Jennifer O'Hanlon née Spring was how they referred to her, because they did not know her by any other name. Her disappearance in 1969 when Martin got six months at Her Majesty's Pleasure guaranteed her place as number one. It didn't change their minds when they learned the truth about bastard husband Martin. No-fault divorce in Australia hadn't arrived by then, so understandably Jen had taken matters into her own hands. She had run away and disappeared after condemning her tormentor to a slow boat to hell. She was it.

Had she taken matters into her hands much earlier, with malice aforethought? Had she started administering a slow solution years earlier? Low-dose strychnine that is. She had to be found. But how? The how and when of her disappearance were quickly established. Many of Jen's former classmates remembered Jen catching a bus to her aunt in Bega.

When interviewed, Aunt Clara from Bega said she had never turned up. There was no reason to doubt her. Her niece's trail seemed to have just washed away. Clever Jen had planned it that way. The detectives cussed and admired her cleverness.

Sergeant Bob suddenly remembered and wrote one of his tables out large on A3 paper. It went up on the corkboard alongside the photos and butcher's papers. It was headed:

NAME BORN MOVED MARRIED SPOUSE BORN

In no time, it resulted in one detective going to Boolaba to interview Mr and Mrs Britten, formerly of Jindabyne.

Bob also pinned up his tables of the scams of 1969 and 1970. This was not really necessary, since he and the detectives agreed that somehow or other the horse rustlings and Martin's demise were related. No one had any idea how this might be so. Bob had checked all the dates and drawn attention to the discrepancies. Hunches were part and parcel of a detective's armoury, but now that was all they had to go on.

The Brittens, Wilson, and Finnbar Mahoney

Homicide Detective Inspector Wilson from Sydney Criminal Investigation Branch called on the Boolaba Brittens at their home, by arrangement of course. He was discretion personified. He wanted to locate a missing person. Could they assist? His discretion was wasted on Eva. 'This is all about the murder of Martin O'Hanlon, isn't it? The Jindy rag is full of it.'

Her perspicacity impressed Wilson. Clearly, he now had to be an open book. Better that than having Eva correct him from in between the lines. He resolved not to put on his clever Dick cap like he did with dumbo interrogees. He played a straight bat instead.

'Now, the Jindy rag has covered in detail the horse rustling case of March this year. They did not take long to link it with a similar case a year earlier. They did not link it to Jennifer O'Hanlon's disappearance in 1969 after the first happening. Nobody posted her as a missing person, so why should they?

'You would understand that our investigations are strictly confidential. You are to tell nobody. We will have press conferences to reveal progress when the time is ripe, or when we appeal for help from the public.'

The Brittens re-told the 1969 events to the best of their recollections. Really there was not that much to tell that had not already been told in the *Cooma-Monaro Express*. Wilson listened carefully, like all good detectives do. Wilson regarded Wilson as a good detective. You did not get to his rank if you were not. It was not an expression of narcissism or self-praise. He had accumulated many notches on his belt with difficult cases solved and the miscreants put away for a very long time. And he wanted one more, from those moon-scape high plains of the Monaro.

He was looking for the littlest detail, the smallest smidgeon, the most personal observation, any change from what others had told him. Or had not told him. He was most interested on her take on the domestic cruelty meted out by Martin on Jen, and her mechanism for coping. Was she a vengeful type? Were there any instances her fighting back? Was Martin ever physical with Jen? Did she ever present to the doctor? Did she confide in her classmates?

'Is there anything else you would like to add,' said Wilson putting his notebook away.

'Well … yes there is, but it might not be relevant.'

Wilson pulled his notebook out again. 'We play longshots as well as the obvious. If it's irrelevant, no matter.'

Eva retold the story of that strange mail she had received, containing just a stamped addressed envelope. After school she had posted it to a local solicitor.

That very evening Wilson was in the Moola Club, as guest of Finnbar Mahoney. This was business to be conducted away from the office. They shared a whiskey as they chatted. Finnbar eschewed whisky, leaving bonny Scots to their wee dram. He ordered full measure, for two, of Ireland's finest. And the rest of the bottle on the table.

Wilson spoke first, revealing his investigation into a murder case in Jindabyne, that he thought the murder was related to the horse thefts, and to the missing person that had no one had seen fit to report.

'Jindabyne. Welln of all of the things that be coming together! Carmel and I have been investigating something else altogether.'

'Who is Carmel?'

'She was my articled clerk for quite a while. She is now a judge's associate in Sydney. She earned her PhD while in my employ. As smart as anyone you will ever meet.'

'I might go and talk to her another time, if you think so highly of her. What were you looking into, and where is it at?'

'It's the curious case of a name change by deed poll. As you just told it came to me via Eva Britten. I lodged it not so long ago. The trouble is, I don't know who it is. Carmel and I did our own detective work – strictly personal, mind – to try to find out. That person was super adept in covering her tracks.'

'A woman. Interesting. We are trying to trace a woman who disappeared in 1969.'

'She had a form for name change completed and witnessed in Jindabyne.'

'Well, I'll be. Under warrant Sergeant Paxton has a copy of Martin O'Hanlon's will. Too bad he never thought to get a copy of the name change by deed poll. Imagine what we could have done with that information. When Harry Lasseter died, the firm's records disappeared. There was no obligation at that time to archive such.

'The will has as beneficiary his wife Jennifer O'Hanlon. And one other in a codicil, I don't remember off hand. Plus a second codicil. That's not important. She disappeared when Martin went to gaol for horse theft. Nobody reported it, because they all thought she had wanted to get away from her husband from hell. They were all on her side. Now, and this part is not out in the public domain, we are investigating Jen for possible murder. The executor just wants to find her to claim her inheritance.'

Finn whistled a bar of 'Danny Boy'. 'It all adds up. You find who has gained a name recently, and you find Jennifer O'Hanlon. To be sure I'm sure of that. Good luck and keep your nose to the stone. Carmel and I have failed to locate Mary Flamboya. At first with that name, we thought maybe she was taking the piss. She had mailed the name change form from Adelaide to the Brittens in Boolaba. Inside another envelope. Eva Britten then posted that inside envelope to us. I completed the registration, and as instructed mailed it to Poste Restante in Alice Springs, c/o Mary Flamboya. Carmel and I came to a dead end. Mary Flamboya for all we know now lives under another assumed name. If so, then what?'

Wilson whistled 'Danny Boy'. Finn smiled at this rendition of his proprietry expression of amazement.

They had both had full measure of Irish ferment. Ah, the real mountain dew of his youth! It took that fair measure to don the wobbly boot, but don they did, Wilson's by far the wobblier. Now all liquored up on Irish single malt, Finnbar turned maudlin. The detective swayed with him, to his hotel, and his drink mate, back home, down winding way. Bachelor Finnbar wiped away a tear, as he couldn't escape the memory.

> *'On October's last*
>
> *I'll fly back home*
>
> *rolling down winding way*
>
> *And all I've got's a pocket full*
>
> *of flowers on my grave*
>
> *But now summer is gone*
>
> *I remember it best*
>
> *Back in the good old world*
>
> *I remember when,*
>
> *she held my hand*
>
> *and we walked home alone in the rain*

how pretty her mouth, how soft her hair

nothing can be the same

and there's a rose upon her breast

where I long to lay my head

and her hair was so yellow

and the wine was so red

back in the good old world'

Tom Waits

The Judge's Associate

Wilson's casual 'I might go and talk to her another time' hadn't fooled Finn one little bit. He was on the blower immediately. Wilson was in the judge's antechamber opposite Carmel Blount as soon as immediately possible – that came as soon she could spare time in her busy schedule. And so it was, when Wilson sat down, she said, 'I've been expecting you.'

'This time I was warned,' mused Wilson. 'Pity I walked into Eva Britten unprepared. What is it about Jindabyne women? Why are they so clever?' They rankled in his bosom, riddled his mind, and addled his brain. He tried not to show how Eva and Finn had delivered a Fools's Mate in this particular chess game. He should have known better. He resolved to make clear that he was the journeyman in this puzzle, and that Carmel had jurisdiction. As if she had to be told. Unusual for him, his ears rang with the music of deference.

Carmel told the little that she knew, plus the lot that she had concluded. Wilson whistled a bar of 'Danny Boy'. Carmel smiled and said, 'Have you been drinking with Finnbar Mahoney?'

She knew how to relax the rather tense Wilson. She guessed, correctly, that Finn had forewarned Wilson what to expect. He had not expected to be run over by a wisdom truck, such a handsome, no, beautiful, one at that. 'Okay. If you were me, where would you start?'

'Well,' said Carmel, 'You have made a good start already.'

She had prodded his ego into life, and then stroked it. Wilson was putty in her hands. Luckily for him, Wilson knew it. Finn had said, 'You are just putty in her hands. Just let her do the kneading.'

'Jeffrey', she said, sliding into familiarity. 'Jeffrey, the last thing you should do is make an appeal to the public, or post up photos of missing persons.'

Wilson hated being called Jeffrey. Carmel knew that. Jeff was okay. But Jeffrey! Sometimes he contemplated even changing his name by deed poll. Nonetheless, he was somewhat flattered that a judge's associate would become familiar with him. Jeffrey said, 'You can call me Jeff.'

Carmel already knew that. Her 'okay, Jeff' completed the seduction, her deliberate behavioural strategy. Wilson was putty in her hands. He underestimated, if he understood at all, her real purpose. It was to disarm him completely and get him to reveal what strictly speaking he should not be revealing. She understood, even at this early stage, that nothing should happen to prejudice a fair trial of Mary Flamboya, the former Jennifer O'Hanlon née Spring. Nothing should leak beyond the police domain for fear that it might become public.

Jeff had indeed intended to post a missing person poster in every police station in the country. He hid that from Carmel, but rightly guessed that she had already concluded that. No matter. Carmel said if you go public, smart Mary/Jennifer will go further underground. We need to take this step by step, don't telegraph anything, and after this meeting, never contact me again. You can catch up with my thinking via Finn. We can safely assume that a Mary Flamboya is not walking the streets in broad daylight. She will have changed her appearance. She will have an assumed name that everyone knows her by. I reckon that she has used this name from the minute she disappeared off the bus in Cooma.

In this she was both wrong and right. Sure their person of

interest used the Flamboya moniker. Plus Jennifer O'Hanlon plus Mary Chiaprisi. But how was Carmel to know that?

'She's obviously clever, and knows that her new name should become second nature to her asap. You don't change it like you change your knickers.'

Jeff hadn't expected to hear the vernacular from a judge's associate. He relaxed some more and used a bit of his own vernacular. 'Some sheila.' Carmel just smiled a gotcha smile. She didn't need dimples. Wilson had no ready smile to smile back with. He was more the domineering kind when trying to elicit information.

'Check all electoral rolls. That's one hell of a job. Just sub-contract it out to state police. I'm sure you can do that with a convincing excuse. You won't find anything, I expect. Finn and I have already checked if Jen voted in the last election. She didn't. Nobody from the Australia Electoral Commission has been able to serve Jennifer O'Hanlon with a please explain or you will be fined.

'Get a copy of Jennifer's New South Wales driver's licence. Check all states' motor vehicle authorities, whatever they are called, if they have issued a driver's licence to a woman born in 1939, between 9 June 1969 and now. That's the day before Jen disappeared. Easy computer job. I don't need to tell you what to do with that list.' That gotcha smile again.

'Check out the owners of all new cars registered from 9 June 1969 to now. You need keep only female owners born in 1939. Easy computer job.

'Check out all transfers of cars to subsequent owners. Ditto who you keep. Easy computer job.

'Check with all states' police if they have issued a traffic breach to a woman born in 1939, between 9 June 1969 and now. Easy computer job.

'Check with the relevant department in each state, for rental agreements lodged between 9 June 1969 and now. You know the drill by now.

'Check with the tax department in each state or whatever it's called, for the tax returns lodged by a woman born in 1939. This is the easiest one. A computer will spit out the answer in no time flat. I expect Jen did not lodge one, not being an official money earner. But you have to do it just in case.

'Check with the taxman in New South Wales for the last ten years' returns for Martin O'Hanlon. You need to know what Martin claimed for his wife. That bastard probably listed her as an employee, deducted dollars as business expenses, even though he paid her nothing apart from doling out the housekeeping money. Did he claim for her after she disappeared?'

'What! A judge's associate happy to talk bastard talk!' Unsaid of course.

'Check with each state authority that registers business names. Check with the registrar of companies, different names in different states, for all companies registered from 9 June to now. A bit later you will have to search them all for owners' and directors' details. That's going to be one hell of a job.'

'All this for one missing person,' moaned Wilson.

'No, this is a murder investigation.'

Shit, thought Wilson, *Did I have to be reminded of that? Lift your game lad.*

'You've got at least six months' work there.'

More like a year, moaned Wilson internally.

'More like a year,' Carmel corrected herself.

She kept her next move to herself. Finnbar would be the first to know. Softly softly catchee monkey.

The Funerals

Martin O'Hanlon had died in April and Harry Lasseter a month later. Martin's body was not released until after his postmortem revealed that he had been murdered. Slow strychnine poisoning. Harry could leave the Cooma morgue immediately. His life had been impeccable. Fat lot of good that did him when the grim reaper came knocking.

Jindabyne did not have a funeral service. They had to use the one located in Cooma, sixty-three kilometres distant. For 'operational reasons' the two funerals were arranged one after the other, one in the Catholic section, the other in the Lutheran section, in Jindabyne Cemetery. For once, the Catholics did not command the best view – they both enjoyed equal oversight of the beautiful Lake Jindabyne. When that high dam wall on the Snowy River was built to hold up the lake, bones buried in Old Jindabyne were relocated, together with the town, to high ground.

The Catholic priest from St Patrick's Church, Cooma, would officiate first. Fitting really, because the family O'Hanlon's Irish forebears had built the first St Paddy's in Cooma in 1861.

For Harry, it would be the pastor from Trinity Lutheran Church. Their little place of worship was built in 1967, in Cooma, designed by a Lithuanian parishioner. That congregation comprised European refugees working on the hydro scheme. By 1971, when Snowy Hydro was complete, sadly the congregation had all but disappeared.

The inhumations were to happen just as the police planned them. Holy moley! The priest never knew that. He only cared that he came first. He had no inkling that the mourners were to be surveilled by the law. The pastor never knew that either. He was happy that Harry's funeral was arranged around his prior commitments. He did not suspect that his pastoral care obligation had been arranged for just the time that Martin was being laid to eternal rest.

No matter that both sets of mourners were one and the same. After all, most of them had church affiliations only for births, deaths and marriages. You could hardly say that Jindabyne was a hotbed of religiosity. No sister city of Lourdes in France.

Wilson was at the Snowy Mountains Airport, fifty klicks from Jindabyne, to see who might land there and then go to the funeral. He watched the little gaggle walk across the tarmac and collect their baggage direct off the trolley. There was no carousel in that small regional airport. He observed a curious thing – one man had boots of noticeably two different sizes. Now any podiatrist will tell you that we are all a little bit off, but not enough that you could pick it in the street.

Wilson followed three hire cars that turned left to Jindabyne, and noted their number plates plus the occupants' appearances.

At the same time, his partner detective Jack Merton went to the Jindabyne airport, light planes only, ten kilometres out of town on Tinworth Drive. Only two Cessnas had lodged flight plans to land there that morning. Merton noted the details of the occupants and followed them both to the cemetery not so far away. Later checks showed they were graziers from out west. Nothing to see there.

It was no coincidence that Wilson arrived from Cooma airport around the same time. They avoided each other. Meanwhile, Sergeant Bob Paxton held fort at the police station. The priest began his service with about fifty mourners by the graveside.

At the same time the pastor had finished his pastoral duty in Cooma and was already speeding to his funeral appointment.

The mourners had just time to don their hats, walk to the Lutheran section, and doff them again, as the pastor began his incantations. Wilson and Merton, socially distanced, noted that the flock had not changed membership. Merton again noticed the man with two-sized boots.

Nobody seemed to notice the two out-of-towners in civilian dress and police issue identical shoes. They were 'in disguise' but instantly recognizable for what they were, so why were they going around trying to look small? They did not show up at the Jindabyne Bowling Club for the wakes. Or should that be wake?

Wilson, Merton and Paxton briefly shared notes in the Jindabyne Police Station in Thredbo Street. The man with two-sized boots went up on the corkboard. Paxton changed into civilians and went to the wake, and to engage with Mr TwoBoots.

This was easy. By now Bob was locally accepted, slapped a few backs on the way to the podium, and got a few slaps himself. He was asked to say a few words. He obliged. He stepped away from the mike and straight to TwoBoots. Hi, I'm Bob Paxton, the new plod here since three months. We haven't met. You from around these parts? Yackety yack.

Bob soon knew quite a bit about him, but not too much. Nothing nosey beyond social chit chat. He moved onto others that he did know and engaged in similar chit chat. TwoBoots saw nothing unusual. Bob was careful to ask others about TwoBoots only when he was beyond earshot. After a socially acceptable time, Bob said his farewells, went back to the police station and pinned up more notes on the corkboard. The detectives went back to their lodgings in the Jindy Inn.

What had the trio learned that day? Only one person had caught the big plane to get to the funeral. The pilots of two light planes also. The commercial plane had flown in on the postman's run from Melbourne, all stops. TwoBoots had joined the flight in Merimbula, with its airport by the golf course, the one famous for its kangaroos on the fairways.

Visiting golfers were told to make sure you respect the old man 'roo guarding his harem on the eighth fairway. It might take a little longer to complete your round. That's better than having to use a No. 1 wood to defend yourself against his attack, his harem's heads turning and their ears twitching in admiration.

Wilson phoned the Merimbula Police next day for intel on Freddy Ford, aka TwoBoots. He was not known to police, in police parlance, and was clean. The only thing of interest was that he was formerly of Jindabyne. He should still have been up on the corkboard.

The name Freddy Ford now went onto the corkboard, but nothing more because there was nothing more. Yet they proceeded with careful absence of carelessness. They asked questions around town about Ford's friends in Jindy in his time there, who he had knocked around with, where had he worked, all the usual stuff. They talked to the aforesaid friends. No, Freddy was not in trouble. We are just building up a complete picture of Martin O'Hanlon, who was just buried as you know. No, he's not in trouble either. We are just building up his complete picture for the coroner.

Bob reckoned it was just like they would have done in a Carribian whodunnit. He didn't say so to the detectives who would have laughed at him, 'Of course this is what we do.'

They next checked on the banking histories of all the faces that graced the corkboard. It had not been hard to source photos of each and every one. No standout transactions, nothing indicating unusual payments to anyone, nothing. A bit disappointing really, because it would have been so good to find blackmail or fraud or grand larceny or such.

The corkboard now had photos in some sort of order. What

was that order? Nobody could verify. It was kind of a reflection of what they thought would best solve the cases – of both murder and horse theft. It was the hunch part of police and detective work. It was pure hunchwork that the two crimes were connected. Well, maybe not pure. If a coincidence is too much to be explained as just fluke, then the balance of probabilities kicks in – there must be some connection, and it needs to be found out.

That photo order was:

Jennifer Spring-O'Hanlon, Freddy Ford, Tom Dooley, Adam Yates, Martin O'Hanlon, Carmel Blount, Finnbar Mahoney, Harry Lasseter, Bill Britten, Eva Rumford.

They added a spiderweb of connecting lines, nowhere near as good as a spider would have spun. Just as good as a Carribian cop would, mused Paxton, but didn't say so out loud for fear of derision from DI Wilson and DS Merton.

The three coppers planned their immediate futures. Bob Paxton had to keep shop in the Jindabyne cop shop. A temporary constable came in to free Bob up from office work to follow up leads. Wilson was off to Moola to see Finnbar. Merton was off to Boolaba to talk some more with Eva and BB. What was their line of attack to be? Two plus two only added up to three so far.

Tom Dooley and TwoBoots

Bob Paxton had by now gained the confidence of that confidence trickster Tom Dooley. As a result, not so smart Tom believed he was in the clear. Paxton let him keep on believing that. 'Tom, let's run through things one more time. You might help me understand what might be missing in the puzzle.' A little flattery goes a long way.

Paxton asked all sorts of innocuous questions about what the school pals did back in the day. He extracted from Tom how he and Eva had liked each other, what they did (carefully excluding theft of vinyl disks), and who else Tom was friendly with among the boys of that age. He operated on the principle: the more I know the less I have to guess.

It was clear that Eva went one way and Tom another, in early 1951. Paxton simply confirmed this, but did not say that his original information came from tittle tattle talk from others. That made Eva an innocent in Tom's future doings, in fact strongly disapproving of anything Tom did after that time. For sure schoolyard talk had kept her up to date.

Paxton steered the talk around to Freddy Ford. He said nothing about the nickname TwoBoots that the police had bestowed on him. He wanted Tom to talk about Freddy off his own bat. 'What sport did you play at primary school?' An innocent enough question.

'Rugby League. There was nothing else in winter, and in

summer we played cricket. Jindy was too small to have its own comp, so we played teams from all around. Cooma was always top dog though.'

'Freddy too?'

'Yeah. We all did. It was kind of compulsory in the school, and anyway we all wanted to.'

'Who provided the gear? Not every family could afford it.'

'The school did. It was always a mad scramble to get the best boots.'

'Who was the best scrambler, and who was the worst.'

'I was the best. Freddy was the worst, because he had to get two pairs. Poor bugger had feet of two different sizes. He hated the nickname we gave him.'

'Like what.'

'TwoBoots!'

Paxton made a mental note for when he would go around searching properties. With a warrant of course. 'What about Adam Yates? Did you knock around with him?'

'Yeah no. You mean Bumfluff. He was a bit, you know, kinda funny. Could hardly read and write. Good bloke though. I used to go with him to properties where he worked after school and holidays 'cause he was a terrific 'orse rider. And good as any rouseabout and a lot cheaper. He used to get his mum to check 'is pay. And he got extra pay for 'is dog that he had trained up.'

'Dog too! What was it?'

'A proper kelpie that rounded up sheep twice as fast. He called it Roadkill. Funny name if you ask me, but that was Bumfluff all over. Ha ha.'

'How the hell do you call a dog called Roadkill to come to you.'

'Oh he didn't call it much. He had lots of different whistles to get him to work the sheep. When the sheep were in a pen, he just called out Roro Roro and the dog knew work was finished for the day. Then 'is head turned outwards and his tail likewise. Bumfluff would hold him in 'is lap.'

'Did Adam count sheep to go to the saleyards?'

'No. He couldn't count properly.'

'So if there were a half dozen horses to get ready for sale, he wouldn't do that?'

'No, somebody else would split the sheep up into whatever yard and do the paperwork. Same with 'orses.'

'I see. I'd better get on with it. Thanks, Tom. See ya.' Paxton wrote up his notes and took Bumfluff Adam's photo off the corkboard and threw it into a drawer.

Then he went out to O'Hanlon's place to search carefully. At the front gate there was blue and white police tape and a sign, 'NO ENTRY'. He didn't know what exactly he was looking for, but it was his job to run over it with a fine-toothed comb. Search as he might, inside there was nothing at all to show that Martin had had any contact with his wife since Jen shot through like a Bondi tram when he went to prison. He made a note that most of her clothes were still in her wardrobe. They were pretty crappy. *I wouldn't want to take them either*, he thought.

Then he walked around the house and outbuildings, looking at the mud that had hardened after the last rains from near a month ago. What the! Baked hard in the mud were many footprints, left right left right – left smaller right bigger!

He took photos with his police camera and notes in his pocketbook. Back in Thredbo Street he finished off his notes after he had checked all rainfall records, amounts and dates. TwoBoots had been around Martin's outbuildings soon after Martin had died, and before the police had had time to make it a crime scene. That had had to wait for the autopsy report.

Paxton and Prey

Paxton went to the lockup room in the police station in Thredbo Street. No, not the one with the bars in it. He went into the one with the corkboard all set up in it, the *Death in Paradise* one he liked to call it. The one with the suspects' parade on it, with its spider webs not as good as a spider's web. For emphasis, he doubled the spider strand between Tom Dooley and, no prizes for guessing, TwoBoots. It was bleeding obvious what he had to do. He phoned the CIB in Sydney, and requested approval for something a bit unusual.

He asked to have Sydney forensics come again to examine the crime scene. He didn't explain. Wilson said what he expected, 'Are you saying that my people are incompetent? Junior officers like you should know their place. It won't look good on your record, bad-mouthing my best forensic investigators. Now, if you have nothing else.'

'Sir, you have to hear me out. I've read their report, which is beyond reproach. I've come across something entirely new.'

'This had better be good. I don't like to have my time wasted.'

'Sir, the report covers only the house.'

'Tell me something I don't already know.'

'That's why I'm ringing you. Down at the stables I've found a set of footprints.'

'Shit, mate. So what?'

'Whoever walked in those boots had feet of two different sizes!'

Wilson pricked up his ears and said, 'You may have something, mate.'

'Sir, the crime scene tape went in two days after Martin died. Nobody since. So TwoBoots must have cased the joint straight away before we got there. We need to find out why, and we need to have the evidence recorded.'

When Paxton explained his new evidence, Wilson agreed forthwith and decided to take credit for this new development. The police were already under internal investigation for the wrongful conviction of Martin O'Hanlon for horse theft from some time earlier. Could this bit of late evidence expose them even further to the vicissitudes of the prying press? He did not relish the prospect of that press conference.

It was cold comfort that the fault for Martin's incarceration lay with the Jindabyne police. In the eyes of the press, they were all in this together. However, in a case such as this, it was fairly standard procedure to announce that new late evidence had come to light. In the same breath the police would appeal to the public to come forward with anything, no matter how small, that might 'help police with their inquiries'.

Now, any number of people may have been to Martin's place for legitimate reasons, read the electricity meter or whatever. But why had TwoBoots been the first? Just two days after Martin's demise. And all the way from Merimbula, over two hours' drive for the near two hundred klicks over Brown Mountain.

Wilson self-praised his own cleverness, forgetting that old adage, 'Self-praise is no recommendation'. To be fair to Wilson, he knew the risk he was taking with this sleight of hand. He also had the standard politician's reply in his back pocket, 'I believed it to be true'. If a polly could hold that line for the Vietnam bombing to rid the world of communism, it would also do to cleanse the soul of the CIB's mini-botched investigation of mere murder.

A late finding of distinctive footprints at the crime scene hardly compared with that lost war. It would not galvanise the masses into another anti-Vietnam War protest march. Like the ones in 1969. It would not.

It would not cause New South Wales premier Askin to repeat in 1973 his infamous 'Drive over the bastards' quip, as President Lyndon Baines Johnston's motorcade was howled at by half a million anti-war Sydneysiders in 1966. That sensitive-souled premier had changed his first name by deed poll from Robin to Robert. Ever so more manly. Ha ha. Move on.

Forensics duly arrived at the crime scene. They were not the same crew as before, so Paxton carefully ran over everything again. He had the previous report to refer to, and the scientists listened intently. They started at the house, begloved and blue plastic booted. Quite logically, that was where the previous examinations had been concentrated. Blue police crime scene tape was still in place. They left their paraphernalia kit boxes with double-hinged lids outside. This time they delved into every nook and cranny. Some took gymnastic skill to reach. For those, it was the job of a lithe twenty-something year-old slim woman.

Samples were carefully bagged, numbered, and locations coded and illustrated on a diagram. She went into the dusty ceiling space and took samples of the dust. They took air samples.

A bit optimistic, thought Paxton, *but thorough wins the day*. He thought of his corkboard back in the lockup. *Just like me.*

By the time the house was done, Paxton produced a picnic hamper, with sandwiches and a thermos flask. The local deli had produced these goodies. Save a drive back into town for victuals.

Paxton's briefing and enthusiasm took on a new fresh turn, nothing to do with that delicious lunch washed down by hot tea. Forensics refrained from smart arse quips of the television crime series kind. But they were just a little bit impressed by what Paxton had unearthed on that hard baked footprinted earth.

Those prints were as distinctive as any left by a peg-legged man. Two distinctly different sized impressions.

They wished for an Aboriginal blacktracker to help with indoor trajectory of these boots. They would just have to do the best they could themselves. Unless. Paxton telepathically volunteered a mate of his, the best horseman around, not to mention hunter of deer that roamed these hills. No show pony. No trick horse.

Albert, known to all and sundry as King, was a neighbour, so was there within the half hour. King relished the task, and Paxton signed him on as temporary police auxiliary. King never walked over any ground without first putting furry big overshoes on. That way his distinctive movements could be easily photographed, along with any others of interest to the assemblage of sleuths.

It was easy in the dried outside mud. After all, dinosaur prints had survived from the Mesozoic to now in mud-turned-rock over two hundred million years, give or take. Inside the yards, he took a minimum number of steps, generally around the edges where nobody usually walked. Kids might stray when playing hopscotch, but not adults. Kids don't step on cracks either. Or hopscotch borders.

Soon they had taken scores of photos, and King had managed to mark on a diagram from where and to where the walker had walked. Impressive. They covered all the area, the round yard, the dressage arena, the high steel yards for the wild ones, and across bare ground to the paddocks down on the lower forty. King pointed out when the walker must have stopped to talk to a truckie. There were single front wheels and one set of double bogie duals, and rear doubles here. These tyres left deeper indents where the truck had parked for quite a while. Probably for loading.

Paxton thought to himself, *Now, why was TwoBoots talking to the truckie?*

'King, are we done?'

'Yeah no. I can't tell you no more. There are lots of other prints, but what use would they be to you? They are all RM Williams work boots. Everybody wears them. An Italian boot salesman would be wasting his time out here. But there is one thing. Somebody wears bloody big RM Williams. Would that interest you?'

'Not really,' was Paxton's opinion.

'Okay, then I'll be off to me day job. The photos should show the big footprints as well as those of TwoBoots. Everyone knows those. If needs be, I can draw you a mudmap of from where and to where big prints had walked. I reckon you could draw that for yourselves. I'll send you a bill. Hose me down. Toodle-oo.'

Merton and the Brittens

Detective Sergeant Jack Merton sat on the veranda with BB after he had finished work in Boolaba. Jack truthfully explained that normal police routine involved building a complete picture of the O'Hanlons. He omitted to say that he was also building a complete picture of everybody that was ever close to Martin and Jennifer. That was no accidental by-product, but he didn't want to reveal just how far the police were prepared to go down this path. That nothing was sacred ground. He was careful however to confine his questions to what BB could tell from first-hand contact with others. He was not interested in third party inadmissible chatter, except to note a follow up with the third person directly involved, if possible.

Fishing often got police into trouble. Jack steered clear of that with BB. It wasn't necessary in any event, because BB was open and honest, and clearly had nothing to hide. He was two years older than Eva, but after they became an item, he had gotten to know her circle of schoolmates. Jack later followed up and chit chatted around them as well. All were honest and open like BB. They too had nothing to hide, but never revealed what each other had said.

It took quite a while before he got onto Freddy Ford, even though Freddy TwoBoots was the main reason for his talking to BB in the first place. Paxton had alerted him to the footprints in the mud, when those footprints should not have been there a few weeks ago.

BB had quite an interesting take on Freddy. He was quite well liked, and played on the school footy team. Boys were graded into two primary school teams – one over seven stone, and the other under. There weren't enough boys for more teams, and girls certainly weren't considered. Freddy was a lump of a lad so played in the same team as BB who was two years older. Tom Dooley too.

When they went to Cooma High School all that changed. The boys were a lot bigger for one thing. There was a lot of bus travel to play other high schools. It was an intermittent competition, with four away games each winter and four at home.

BB reckoned Freddy was a bit secretive, kept things to himself, and avoided talking about things the other kids did. Nobody quite knew what Freddy did after school and on holidays. He never did anything wrong, not like Tom Dooley, who was plain shifty.

Freddy marched to the sound of a different drum. About chemistry classes Eva had complained to BB that he was always doing experiments they were told not to. More than once the lab had to be evacuated because of what Freddy's test tube emitted. Hydrogen sulphide and such. Jack made a mental note to follow up separately with Eva, who had just arrived home from Moola, relieved to have survived another day's teaching. Those kids!

Jack diplomatically thanked BB, said he would chat to Eva, and that he wouldn't keep him from all the other things he had interrupted. Eva knew DS Merton would not be talking to them as a couple. In any event BB didn't want to sit through the same stuff again.

Jack wanted to quickly brush over Eva's classmates of those years ago, because there was nothing to see there except Freddy Ford and of course Jennifer Spring. 'Where should I start?' A rhetorical question to which Jack had never in his career expected an answer.

Eva said, 'Let's we get straight to the point. Let's start with Freddy Ford!'

Jack felt as though he had been caught snoring in a concert. He hadn't met Eva and her formidable intuitions before. Wilson should have said to him, 'Welcome to the sisterhood, Jack. Now mind your Ps and Qs.' He hadn't. Wilson likewise had had no intention of saying, 'And wait until you meet her classmate Carmel Blount.' He wanted Jack to experience that encounter totally unprepared. Eh eh.

Eva was well ahead of her interrogator. She understood that the most important questions would normally be coming last from the Sydney detective. She could read him like an open book, even though in interviews Jack presented as a closed book, or at least an opaque one. Eva didn't want to waste time. She had nothing to hide. She had plenty to illuminate.

'As you wish, Eva. Freddy Ford first it is then.' He was taken aback and ever so slightly off balance, thinking, *And this is what detectives are trained to do to their interrogees! Not have others do unto you. Okay, let's get this over and done with.*

Eva said, 'Let's get this over and done with. I'll tell you everything relevant about Freddy Ford and if I miss anything you can bring me up to speed!' Jack Merton was like putty in her hands.

'Freddy Ford was a likeable boy, a big lump of a lad. Played a good game of football right from primary school, and on in high school. He was Cooma High's star player. And he had feet of two different sizes. Poor TwoBoots copped that from all sides. Cooma cheer squad on one side and the opposition on the other snarling "TwoBoots" at him. He never reacted but I know he was hurt from both sides, but never showed it. He was secretive, hid things from others, looked guilty a lot but what for I don't know. Still waters run deep, you might say. But what direction Freddy's mind ran was beyond me. He was a hard box to open.'

Jack hoped his gob-stopped didn't show.

'I don't know what you know, DS Merton, but if it's half what I know then no wonder he is a prime suspect of yours for something or other.' Jack didn't rise to the bait, which was what Eva expected. It didn't stop her from trying again.

'Freddy seemed to be in Jindabyne always around the same time each month. He wasn't that close to his family, so twelve visits a year is fair enough I figure. But why wasn't it on weekends?' Jack's eyes rounded only momentarily, but Eva registered it in the same instant. 'DS Merton, you wouldn't be interested in what days he showed up would you?'

Jees, thought Jack, *Do you have to round me up like Bumfluff's kelpie, Roadkill?* He thought he'd call check in this little chess game. 'Bet you think I would say "Cooma sales day." '

'I knew you would,' said Eva ever so sweetly. 'Aren't you going to write that down in your notebook? Now let's get onto Jennifer.'

Jees, thought Jack, *she's giving me a right royal doing over.* He hoped it didn't show. Hope springs eternal and Eva smiled her knowing smile. That rubbed it in even more, and she didn't need to say a single bloody word. *OMG, she reads me like an open book. I am putty in her hands.*

Eva check-mated Jack with, 'You really should talk to my ex-classmate Carmel Blount. She would be most helpful, I'm sure.'

Mentally, Jack prostrated his queen on their imaginary chess board.

'But I'm sure that your colleague will do just as well.'

They talked over and under and around Jen's disappearance from when Martin went to gaol. It threw no further light, and Eva apologised for it. 'I'm sorry to be of no use about Jen. Martin shut her off from the world as soon as they were married. Jen's bubbles and smiles and dimples disappeared, just like that. She was clever at school, and I reckon that she had planned her disappearance down to a T. She let on to nobody. When she left, we were all on her side. Still are. Only one thing – it's hard to believe she's a murderer.'

'We are mystified,' said Jack. For once Eva could only agree.

That evening, Jack rang Wilson for a debrief. 'Now you know all that I have pieced together. One final thing – the missing woman is all smiles and dimples.

Softly Softly

Judge's Associate Carmel knew that she herself couldn't directly uncover the whereabouts of Mary Flamboya. It wasn't about conflict of interest. Her mentor judge would never be presiding over the trial of whoever was the murderer of Martin O'Hanlon. She was proper about keeping her work away from her other life. She left her work at the wood-panelled legal chambers at each day's end. Yes, Carmel had another life outside. She hadn't had one until she became Carmel Blount PhD. She was just careful not to bring her other life to her work.

She knew how she could go about uncovering the unknown's whereabouts. She could not officially work on the case, but there was nothing to prevent her thinking about it. Also, her thought processes were so fast that it didn't take her long to come to conclusions, to know what to do next.

Carmel herself may not have been able to sleuth, but she had the agency of her former boss, the redoutable Finnbar Mahoney. They were on the phone weekly, always at the same time, always starting with the same topic – where oh where could Mary Flamboya, or more to the point her alias, be?

They always agreed that there were two lines of attack. One line just might lead to Mary Flamboya. This would demand thorough regular searches. The detectives would be doing that already. Not much point in duplicating their investigations. Besides, Carmel had already given Wilson a fulsome list of things that they must do. One thing not – post missing persons photos in every police station in the land. That would drive the target further underground. That would have to be much later in the hunt. If at all.

There was another line might unearth what's-her-name. Carmel surmised that finding her would take cunning and guile, not just trawling through official records. And who's to say that her name might come to light too late, before she adopted another alias? The detectives, thanks to DS Jack Merton, knew one thing that Finn and Carmel did not. Their quarry was all smiles and dimples!

Finn, advised by Carmel, refrained from contacting Wilson for updates. He kept an eye on the press, following on from her thinking that at some stage the police would be appealing to the public. He speculated on what form that appeal might take. If it was to help with a murder case, that would send a warning to the missing Mary just as surely as if they had posted photos of her in all police stations in the land. Surely the cops wouldn't do that!

Or if it was to ask the public for information leading to the arrest of horse rustlers, then that was another thing altogether. That just might bear fruit, because the wider public were in no way aware that the police connected horse theft and murder. Jennifer what's-her-name might be the only person to know the answer to that conundrum. And even she might not know, if she were innocent. Police suspicions were just that. Proof was a quantum leap away. Carmel and Finn shared this opinion. They would just wait. And wait.

Little by little their regular phone chats took on another hue. Both looked forward to Monday evenings at 7:00, after dinner dishes had been washed. There was nothing much on the three television channels on Mondays. Bit by bit, some small talk mixed in with their sleuthing. The chats gradually grew longer than was strictly necessary. Put it down to Finnbar's having kissed the Blarney stone if you must. Carmel was of course more economical with her words, with the worth of her each word proportionally higher than Finnbar's.

Finn's were more entertaining, if a transcript were ever to be produced. The interplay of gregarious and circumspect, the talkative and the economical, the light-hearted and the straight, would have intrigued any playwright. Add in flashes of Irish humour, and a two-hour theatre experience would be guaranteed.

Weeks had passed by. One Monday chat opened with, 'Carmel, did you see ...?'

Carmel answered Finn in mid-sentence, 'The *Sydney Morning Herald* and the *Cooma-Monaro Express*! Plus Australia wide!!! We were right. *"Horse rustling has become a serious business in the Monaro. The public are invited to submit any information that might assist the police. Telephone the Sydney Flying Squad at (02) xxxx xxxx. Remember, your horse could be next."* '

Neither was impressed with this public notice; both thought that they could have drafted much better. It didn't matter, because the authors were not all that interested in horses. The police were much more interested in catching a monkey. And this notice, bound to have come to the attention of Mary Flamboya, would have the desired effect of lowering the monkey's caution. She would relax her guard just a tad, because horse theft was the last reason why anyone would be searching for her. Or so the cops thought. Two others and Mary thought otherwise.

Carmel was always careful to share credit with Finn, no matter she thought of something first. Finn behaved the same. *We* always came up with ideas. It was now time to reveal her hand to Finn. Softly softly catchee monkey. Finn whistled a bar of 'Danny Boy'.

'Finn, it's time *you* put an entry into the *Law Society Journal*. *We* can draft it. It's most unlikely that any member of the public reads our *Journal*. It will alert solicitors around the country to exercise their minds on our challenge.' This is what 'we' drafted:

'A person disappears without trace. All usual search avenues have failed. Our practice has performed a routine legal task. No red flag

attaches. It would usually be filed and forgotten. The former name has been carefully hidden by a series of steps involving multiple solicitors. Unregistered mail postmarked various states has been sent without return address. The final executed name change by deed poll was mailed to Poste Restante Alice Springs for collection. It doesn't mean the legal Mary Flamboya picked it up in person. Would any solicitor contact Mahoney & Geeves, Moola Moola, NSW with any information that might uncover the whereabouts of Mary Flamboya.'

They knew solicitors would be intrigued by poor language and the total lack of legalese. Let them figure out why. They didn't expect, nor did they get, any quick replies. Then one Monday evening at seven on the dot, Finn said, 'Got one.' He ran through the reply that came via the solicitors' courier bag. Not the *Law Society Journal*. He was a bit puzzled as he read it.

'Congratulations on a pseudo legal problem that no firm would do pro bono for a private person. I have taken up your gauntlet here in Brisbane. My thinking might lead you to a solution. It might not. Either way there is no charge.

Preliminary work suggests that Mary Flamboya is not likely found in Brisbane. In due course you might let me know where my suggestion leads, if anywhere.

I have gone through the history of this case. It was not that hard to get, even if you chose not to divulge. I have searched the usual official records that any solicitor would use to advise on a missing person's case. Someone is no doubt already doing that. Mary Flamboya hasn't left a trace via driver's licence, car rego, that sort of thing. Easy enough to get around, and she sounds plenty clever enough.

Let's start with the assumption that clever Mary would want to start a business. With her brain, how could she fail? With the memory of her husband stuck firm in her head, she's unlikely to work for someone else. No, she's calling the shots somewhere.

We don't know what alias she used from the day she disappeared. We probably never will, if she changed it again. Now, here's my theory for what it's worth.

She has acquired an off-the-shelf company through an accountant. Interstate, I would vouch. No lawyer involved. There are thousands such created in Australia each year. A company search is impractical for all of Australia. You don't know the name, and even if you did, you can bet Mary Flamboya is not a director.

I'm also confident that she would be setting up a holding company, making things even harder.

She probably did the two company structures in two different states. Under the Corporations Act 2001 what works in one state holds good in another. Good luck. My pro bono stops here.'

Finn thought it was a rather wishy-washy reply, and not all that helpful. But then their request had been the same. Why should he not return serve with backhand pace and top spin? Carmel thought with her usual quick, and whistled a bar of 'Danny Boy'.

'You know, Finn, he does have something. *We* haven't thought of her using a holding company structure to hide the beneficial owner of her business. I've got another thought as well.'

'Pray tell. What have we gained? Searching holding companies has narrowed the field? Not much.'

Carmel had thought of that too. She said, 'What does Mary Flamboya telegraph her punches with?'

'Got me,' conceded Finn.

'Well, Jen O'Hanlon disappears from New South Wales. My hunch is that you can discount her setting up business in our state. It increases the risk of someone recognising her. Brisbane's out; we just have to accept our "legal" advice from there. He's got our number. We didn't fool him. Or could that be a her?

'Then she used Adelaide to post a letter to you, via BB and Eva in Boolaba. I think it's a safe bet she chose that name randomly from a phone directory. Same goes for you as choice of solicitor. She doesn't know you, so I infer she didn't know who Mrs W Britten of Emerald Street Boolaba was either. Are you with me?'

Finnbar changed his tune. He whistled a bar of the 'Hallelujah Chorus'. Satan and all his minions gloriously arrayed! 'Crikey, Carmel. I'm with you. So she doesn't live in Adelaide.'

'The last pieces of the puzzle come from her choice of Alice Springs for Poste Restante. What a blue-arsed fly, eh? She doesn't live in the Alice. Too small a place anyway to set up shop as well. That leaves Melbourne and Perth.

'Melbourne is the manufacturing hub of Australia, even if it does run second to Sydney as a financial centre. Melbourne is harder to break into. Old money talks louder there. Ergo, our Mary lives in Perth. Big enough to get lost in, small enough to have lots of business growth as mining takes off with a vengeance there. I'd take a punt on Mary being a Perth girl now.'

'Do we tell the detectives to search holding companies in Perth? If *we* try to do that ourselves, *we* risk stepping on police toes. I have said softly softly catchee monkey, and I still think so. I think there is one thing we can do without upsetting our friends Wilson and Merton.'

Finn contacted Wilson, 'Search holding companies in Perth.' He left it cryptic. He did not reveal who they should be searching for.

'It's time we laid out a bait that Mary what's-her-name might just take. We're within our rights to do it. I think we should place a discreet ad in *The West Australian*. The wording should be vague. Mary should know it is aimed at her, letting her know we think that she lives in Perth.' Mahoney & Geeves placed the following in the 'Public Notices' section of *The West Australian* and only in *The West Australian*:

'All persons having an interest in the Estate of Martin O'Hanlon late of Jindabyne New South Wales please contact (01) ZZZZ ZZZZ for advice that you may be to your advantage. Probate may be granted when all responses have been considered.'

The code could not have been clearer. The cops back east would not have read it.

I am Woman

'I am woman, hear me roar

In numbers too big to ignore

And I know too much to go back an' pretend

'Cause I've heard it all before

And I've been down there on the floor

No one's ever gonna keep me down again'

Helen Reddy

Mary Chiaprisi Flamboya O'Hanlon Spring duly read that small public notice in *The West Australian*. She recalled the earlier Sydney Flying Squad notice in the national press calling for assistance in combatting horse theft. She let her thoughts wash over her brain. Surely it was no coincidence that the will advertisement appeared so soon after the yihaa about horse theft? And only here in the west?

She pondered the telephone numbers of both. She dialled the Flying Squad number and fed them some bumfluff about having had a horse stolen recently. When they asked for her details, she hung up. She confirmed that that disingenuous notice was at least genuine. The Jindabyne police were baiting her.

She wondered out loud, 'Why did the number (02) ZZZZ ZZZZ not also give the name of the law firm that had posted it in the paper? Do they think me ingenuous?'

It took her no time flat to hatch a plan. She could hardly go to the Perth GPO and scan through every phone number in every business directory in the land. But she could peruse the Moola Moola yellow pages!

It had to have come from there. What other solicitors had she contacted? None. It seemed so obvious, but obviously it hadn't registered with Mahoney & Geeves! And so by day's end Mary had assured herself that M & G had placed the ad. And she knew which identity she would use when she replied. Bring it on!

Mary wanted to put a bit of daylight between notice and her making contact. She waited another fortnight. Let M & G stew for that while.

During those two weeks she made sure that Joe Martinelli had followed up on each business lead that Mary conjured. She certainly had a business brain. She would show M & G the right side of her brain before too long. Mary decided that it was time that Italian espresso coffee machines appeared in all pubs and clubs and sandwich shops and bakeries. Faema, Illy or Lavazza. No matter which. And by the time she finished, there would not be too much wriggle room for opposition newstarts.

She told Joe about the building she had bought in trendy Subiaco.

'Why there?' asked Joe. 'You could just buy a cheaper warehouse in an industrial estate. Why so big? A quarter or half at the outside would do.'

'I know,' said Mary. 'But I have other things in mind.' Mary explained. Joe whistled his admiration at her acumen. He would organise some Sicilian mates to do the fitout, exactly according to instruction. It would be ready in a month, if they worked day and night.

'Yes please,' came from Mary. Joe knew without being told that he was being told to get cracking. Joe was to install industrial coffee roasting and grinding equipment, the best that Italy could supply. He was to arrange for a range of coffee paraphernalia to be stocked.

'Joe, I want you to recruit a warehouse manager for when it opens. You have too much on your plate already. I know you will find a good, reliable one. No need to go to an employment agency. The same goes for a sales assistant. This time I want our receptionist involved with you.

'Oh. I nearly forgot. We need a good barista, someone who can teach others and who can present coffee tastings for the general public. Think how cellar doors operate in the vineyards and wineries.'

The receptionist would also make sure to have new business cards printed, with the Subiaco address as 'company headquarters'. Mary asked to have a photo of the building as background on the card, just as soon as the 'Forza Coffee' sign had been mounted. It was carefully designed to complement the Subiaco atmosphere. That suburb was already trendy, and Mary sensed that this was only the beginning.

Finally, print a thousand business flyers. Here is the proof copy. Forza Coffee headquarters prominent. And her personal mail was to be re-addressed from PO Box to the warehouse address. She didn't offer any reason. Her staff knew better than to question any decision. They were always consulted on changes that affected them, so no reason to query.

Self-starter Joe hit the road with a vengeance. This time it was to pubs, clubs, and bakeries and sandwich shops. And organise take away cups for all our customers, with Forza Coffee on the side. And I want you to have keep cups on sale. That way we can avoid more rubbish and it would make a good ad campaign for us. Nobody has thought of it yet.

He was also to offer Forza caps and aprons to all their customers, free of charge. And shower caps! With a coffee bean on them! Has this girl lost the plot?

With existing businesses Mary did the same follow up, all charm and dimples, just to make sure Forza's long and growing customer list was happy. The smallest complaint – she called them suggestions – were addressed within the next business day.

Next business day was beginning to be next day, whatever that day was, as all over Australia, weekend trading was being introduced. State governments were passing new trading legislation. Local councils decided that pavement cafes would not lead to epidemics. Europe after all had not had plagues for centuries in spite of summer pavement cafes.

Canberra started it. A real surprise because the Department of the Interior had always resisted, arguing that those 'Canberra canaries' will kill you if you have a coffee on the pavement! Those flies that get up your nostril as you jog for exercise won't hurt you in that environment. But they would on a pavement. Go figure! Gus's café was given the first permit, conditional on a kind of room being built on the pavement. No walls, no roof, no barrier to flies. It was 1971. That incongruous ugly steel structure still stands, much loved curiosity, probably heritage listed.

Mary told Joe that he was in charge for an extended time, maybe a month, as she took a break. Well-earned, she said, 'But I'll be checking out what's new back east.' More likely she was checking how far ahead she was.

That night she went to the Italo Australian Club. It was not a night for Tarantella. That was only for fiestas. It was slow music night. That suited her mood perfectly. She needed to hear herself think. Joe was there as well, this being a sort of send-off. Mary made sure to save the last waltz for Joe.

She rang a real estate agent in Jindabyne and rented a house for a few days. There were plenty to be had in summer, not so many in ski season when you needed to book well in advance and hope the snow was there for your booking. Mary booked it in the name of Jennifer O'Hanlon!

Then she rang Mahoney & Geeves in Moola Moola. 'I'd like to engage a solicitor please.' The receptionist put the call through to Finn. 'Why, to be sure I can do your legal work for you. Who would I speaking to?'

'Mary Flamboya! I believe you know who I am even though we have never met.'

Sweet Jesus and Holy Mother of Mary, went through Finn's head. *I need to kiss the blarney stone again, that'd be for sure. Would there be no end of clever women in my life? If it's not raining at eight, I'm sure to be soaking by nine.*

Mary had expected a stunned silence, but not this long. 'Why would you be so surprised? I expect you'd feel vindicated by your perspicacity in finding Mary. I'll be over east for a while attending to business, and I need some advice.'

She lingered over the words 'over east' to confirm in code that Finn had been clever.

Not as clever as you, passed unsaid through Finn's head. *This will be some chess game. I wonder what she is playing at? Clearly she wants me to play. I can't refuse. I've got too much skin in the game,* he rightly thought.

'I knew you would love to be my advisor. That's why I decided it should be you. Better a lawyer with some skin in the game, I say.'

Finn counted the five women whose cleverness he feared. Jennifer Spring – O'Hanlon. Madame what's-her-name. Mary Flamboya. Carmel Blount. Eva Rumford – Britten. He never realised that five was really three. The first three were one and the same. And there was still one missing – Mary Chiaprisi.

He checked with his receptionist and made an extended appointment for Tuesday one week hence. He could have done it sooner, but he wanted to talk to Carmel first. Monday's phone call was still six days away. Finn knew better than to ring busy Carmel any other evening. Even for an event such as this.

Come Monday, the talk was all business. No social chit chat as per recent normal. Carmel whistled 'Danny Boy', Finn a bar of the 'Hallelujah Chorus'. They both giggled but not for long. Where was this leading? Their combined thinking didn't lead very far. Carmel for once could proffer no advice on how to prepare for the coming assignment with the formidable Mary Flamboya. Finn would just have to wing it. Carmel's final advice was, 'Say a few Hail Marys at the start.'

Finn had trouble concentrating on his other cases. Tuesday dawned bright and sunny, just as it always was for the most part out west. There was a thunderstorm in his head as the appointed nine o'clock arrived.

Finn had not expected the smiles and dimples that charmed him from across the table. Nor the innocuous nature of the advice Mary Flamboya sought. He just thought how much her voice sounded like her smile and how her smile was her dimple's twin.

She said mysteriously that her interest in the will would involve a visit to the police. That's where Mr Mahoney came in. She formally addressed Finn like this, in spite of all his protestations to the contrary. Clearly to him she was maintaining a distance.

The appointment with the police was made for the next Monday, giving them an easy drive across the western plains, and a nine o'clock start in Jindabyne. She didn't talk much.

Pity the Plod; or,
'Murder, she Cried!'

They walked into the Jindabyne Police Station, a little before nine, solicitor Finnbar Mahoney a respectful step behind his client. Sergeant Bob Paxton asked what he could do for him. First mistake.

'For me, actually,' she said, taking in his name tag.

'Sorry.'

'Why is it that men always make assumptions? Do you think I am just a decoration?'

'Sorry again.'

'Bob, stop saying sorry all the time. I'm not going to bite you,' said with sudden offputting familiarity.

Finn was not so sure but only said, 'I'm her advising solicitor.'

Paxton now waited until spoken to. 'You had better ask who I am,' she said, all smiles and dimples. It was Paxton's turn to whistle under his breath. He would recognise those smiles and dimples anywhere, even though he had never seen them before.

'To you, Sergeant Paxton, I am Jennifer O'Hanlon.' Formal again. Finn nearly folded at the knees.

'To my solicitor Mr Mahoney here, I am Mary Flamboya.'

This time Finn asked for a chair to sit on. Paxton responded by saying, 'We had better go into an interview room. This might take some time. Can I get you a coffee?'

Jennifer, known alias Mary Flamboya and unknown alias Mary Chiaprisi said, 'I hope it's a good coffee. No Nescafe instant for me,' knowing full well that instant coffee it would be.

When it came in, she said, 'You really must install a Faema office mini. You'd be ever so much happier with the brew. So would this poor unfortunate you have to interview, solicitor by side.'

Finn wriggled a little in his seat. He could see who was boss at this little gathering. Paxton's discomfiture was writ large on his face.

She said nothing about also being Mary Chiaprisi. They need never know, at least until they found out for themselves. And by then it wouldn't matter. Mary threw down the gauntlet square at Paxton's feet, 'Tell me what you have found out about horse rustling?'

Paxton gathered all the authority that his police badge could muster. 'I ask the questions. You just answer.'

'Very well, *SERGEANT PAXTON*. Ask away. I've got all day. I'm paying Mr Mahoney by the hour. And I'm paying for you in my taxes. I hope you deliver good value for taxpayer's money.'

Finn wriggled some more. Only Mary noticed. But she also noticed that Paxton hadn't noticed. But she noticed that Paxton sat a little less upright opposite. She flicked her dark hair back over her right shoulder. Arched an eyebrow. Both men certainly noticed Jennifer now.

Finnbar drew a little comfort from the fact that now there were only four women whose cleverness he feared. He wondered why Mary/Jennifer was holding court at the Police Station, and what hoped she to achieve?

'When did you find out that Martin O'Hanlon was stealing horses?'

'I found out he was innocent the day the Cooma Court found him guilty! Jindy folk came to the same conclusion, bit by bit, when it became bleedingly obvious that he could not have committed the theft. The police never wanted to find out the truth because it exposed their poor investigation work. You were only interested in fingering a "guilty" someone. Looks good on your crime stats!'

Finnbar thought, *I could have forewarned you, but I'm glad I didn't. Anyway, you are not my client.*

Paxton sat a little lower. Jennifer looked demure, no smile, no dimple. Next, he asked, 'Do you have any idea who might have done it?'

Finn interrupted, 'Hearsay is not admissible as evidence. I advise her not to reply.'

'Advice heeded.'

Jennifer/Mary put on her straight face. 'I do not have the authority to interview suspects. The police do. You may choose whether or not to tell us what you know. So let's move on, shall we?'

Paxton felt as though he was being rounded up by Roadkill, that famous kelpie of Adam Yates. What a name for a dog. He pressed on. 'Why didn't you appear as a witness at your husband's trial?'

'Because when police were putting together a case, they could see that I was not involved. Besides, I was doing what my bastard of a husband always made me do. Shut up. He kept me in the dark like a mushroom. When he spoke to me it was only to find fault. And you expect that, somehow, I could stand up in court and find words to vindicate him. Of anything. Including wrongful police prosecution. Give me a break.'

'What made you conclude at the trial that Martin was innocent, in spite of being "such a bastard"?'

Finn refrained from advising Mary to decline to answer. She did, in her own inimitable way. 'That's for me to know, and you to find out.'

'But we already know why, embarrassing as it is for the police. You would know I was in Sydney at the time. The investigators involved have been demoted. So why won't you tell me how you knew?'

This time Finn advised her not to answer. She did anyway. Finn had to admire her answer, that left Paxton in no doubt. 'What, just to confirm police incompetence? Or more to the point, corruption?'

'Let's move on. Why did you choose to disappear? Where did you go? It makes you look guilty of something.'

'I wanted to get as fast and as far away as possible from the shitty life I had here for ten years. No friends. No visitors. No social life. Kept like a slave. No future. No prospects. Enough said, Sergeant Paxton?'

'Okay. That's clear. But where did you go?'

'Look. When I left, I did not want Martin to find me. Ever. I'm sure you don't blame me. You would have heard from everybody that you have interviewed that Martin was the husband from hell. Mr Mahoney here worked out where I went. He was my lawyer in a way, even if he didn't know it at the time. I'm instructing him now that our client/lawyer business is confidential. I can assure you this – it is not material to your horse theft case. Isn't that so, Mr Mahoney?'

Finn could only nod in agreement. 'I must keep my client's business with me totally confidential.'

'Now, may I make a comment without you asking me a question first?'

Paxton was beaten, 'Yes, go ahead, if it is in some way relevant.'

'I do not appreciate the police fishing for something against me.

Why did the Sydney Flying Squad place an ad in the national press, all around Australia, about horse rustling in the Monaro? How the hell could someone in Coober Pedy help with horse theft in Jindy? I'll tell you why. You wanted to flush me out. As if this pathetic ad would do it. You no longer had any need to flush me out for information on horse theft. You were trying to fry a different fish altogether.'

'Okay. I've let you express an opinion. Now what on earth could the ulterior motive be?'

'Murder! I am a person of interest. "Helping the police with their inquires" is the term, I believe.'

Finnbar swallowed a whistle, of 'Danny Boy' and the 'Hallelujah Chorus'. Sweet Mary and Joseph and Jesus too! *Where is Carmel when I need her?*

He said, 'This is an interview of a different magnitude. I need more time to confer with my client. Could we meet again tomorrow, shall we say ten o'clock?' Finn had a fair idea that the morrow's interview would see a surprise sprung by the sergeant. He said nothing.

Jindy Digs

Jennifer said, 'I have rented a nice house in Jindabyne. There is a spare bedroom for you. That way you won't have to bill me for accommodation. That is, unless I bill you, and then when you bill me, I pay you.'

Finn said with a laugh, 'You're talking Irish to the Irish, I hope you know. But would there be an angle even an Irishman can't see?'

'Well, if I charge you nothing, then it's a gift in kind. Not illegal, just hospitality. The marginal cost of this gift is zero to me, because I am renting the house anyway. And for all you know it might be a legitimate tax deduction for me. So no skin off my nose.

'On the other hand, if I charge you and you pay me, it's taxable income for me, and tax deductible for you. I'm worse off, unless my accountant can work out how rental income is not part of my taxable income, and thus not lodged.

'You're better off, because you have increased your allowable deductions. And there's one more angle. Can you think of it, Mr Mahoney?'

'I'm a lawyer not an accountant. I don't even understand double entry bookkeeping.'

'If I charge you and you pay me, then the gross national product is increased by the amount that I charge you and that you pay me. So it gets counted twice. And yet national welfare is exactly the same whether the GNP is enhanced or not. Isn't that interesting?'

'If you say so. Should I call you Jennifer or Mary?'

'Neither.'

'What then?'

'Jen. And do you mind if in private I call you Finnbar?'

'Yes, I do mind.'

'What then?'

'Finn.'

Both agreed that it was better not to artificially inflate the GNP. In return, Finn would pay for the chew and spew they took home. Not much good food had hit Jindabyne by the early seventies. Both agreed that that arrangement also prevented double counting in the GNP. As if. Both chuckled, Jen more than Finn. He knew once again when he had been done over by a superior intelligence.

It was only confirmed by what Jen said next. 'Finn, after we have eaten and burped our appreciation, I'll leave you time to talk to your collaborator on the phone. I had this line hooked up for a few days for my use. Tax deductible and all. I'll step outside for fresh air for fifteen minutes. That should give you time to better prepare for my police interview tomorrow.'

'Why do you think I have a collaborator?'

'Because no man on his own would have worked out that Mary Flamboya lived in Perth!'

Finn hid his hurt feelings so well that eagle eyes herself didn't know the hurt she caused. In any event, Finn's feelings didn't come into it. His hurt was hugely outweighed by the benefit of getting fifteen minutes' worth of Carmel's wisdom.

After dinner, after Finn's phone call to Carmel, and after the takeaway cartons were in the bin, Jenn offered a glass of the finest Irish whiskey, one lump of ice. She partook of a gin and tonic, no ice. One was all she allowed. They had to keep a clear head for the morrow. Their preparation would be a little more relaxed as they sipped.

'Jen, I don't have to tell you that we must be super careful in choosing our words in tomorrow's interrogation. I'm sure you know you and murder are the subject of interrogation, whatever spin Paxton may place on it. You will be doing all the talking, and I will interrupt as often as necessary. Strictly on legal points. I have no intention of gagging you. A bit depends of course on what you tell me tonight.'

Jen said, 'I'm with you, and I'm glad you are my advisor, plus someone else unknown that you think is even better than you. Can I ask who that someone is?'

'Well, not really. Strictly speaking, my collaborator is doing it pro bono.'

'Finn, why are you being evasive with me?'

Spare me, thought Finn, then out loud, 'Because there is a potential conflict of interest that must be avoided at all costs. That's why my evasion, as you call it.'

'Fair enough, Finn. That makes her a legal person in a place that needs to be strictly independent, at least for the outside world to see.'

'Yep. Can we leave it at that?'

'Well, no.' A dramatic pause. 'You see, I already know!'

'Dare I ask,' slunk Finn.

'Carmel Blount!'

Finn had run out of tunes to whistle. Instead he just asked lamely, 'How?'

'Finn, it's plain as the nose on my face. I guess you haven't noticed that either. Is it straight or just the weeniest bit aquiline?'

'It's pretty. That's all I can say.'

'I thought so. I won't think any the less of you though. It's actually quite a nice thing you just said. Makes me feel more confident.'

As if, thought Finn.

Jen said, 'I thought you'd think that.'

They both laughed long and hard.

'Well, it's like this. I was around when Carmel was Harry Lasseter's receptionist. She was there when I went for my change of name by deed poll. Harry did it on the spot, and gave me my copy. When I disappeared – pretty successfully, I think you'd agree – Carmel would have put two and two together. Harry, too. But he died before he could come up with the answer four.

'I knew that Carmel went to law school in Sydney, but I had not been close to her ever since I married that bastard Martin. I guessed that someone would have told Carmel as soon as I disappeared. If not, she would certainly know when the shit hit the fan about Martin's murder.'

'Did you know Carmel worked for me after graduation?'

'No.'

'Then why associate her with me?'

'Elementary my dear Watson. By the ad you put in *The West Australian*, inviting me to hear something that might be to my advantage. How could Mahoney & Geeves possibly know about an obscure will in Jindabyne unless someone from there told you. There could only be one somebody. QED.'

Finn declined Jen's invitation to whistle something. He just exhaled long and slow without pursing his lips. He luxuriated in the aroma of the whiskey as he drew breath back in.

'And you'd figured out that I lived in Perth. Why else was that ad only in *The West Australian*? Now, let's get down to business.'

'Jen, you probably have come to this conclusion already. You won't be facing Sergeant Paxton tomorrow. It will be Sydney detectives Wilson and Merton.'

'I knew that as soon as Paxton made the appointment for ten in the morning. The plane from Sydney lands at Cooma-Snowy Mountains Airport at nine. It is about fifty klicks away, perfect for a ten start.'

'Again, Jen, you'll be doing all the talking when questioned. My first bit of advice is to not offside them. You got the better of Paxton, and I'm sure that you are more than a match for these two. You know no doubt that they have had long sessions with myself and Carmel. What you might not know is that she certainly got the better of them, so you don't have to repeat the dose.

'You might say something to them to get Pavlov's dog's response. That should be enough to stop their well-known tactic of good cop bad cop. You just don't want to provoke bad cop. I know you can handle anything that bad cop can throw at you – that's not it. I just tink you need to keep your powder dry and not give too much away with a clever reply that might backfire.'

'Don't worry, Finn. I will be decorum personified.'

'Now, you must have something in your locker. Or should I call that armoury? Why do you volunteer to come to the police when it was doubtful that they could have uncovered you?'

'Well, let me put it like this. I know I did not poison Martin. I know they would have me up on their corkboard, with an out-of-date photo, with spider lines connecting me to other persons of interest. I know that no self-respecting spider would spin such a web. I saw the web the cops spun to put Martin into the Cooma lockup for something he couldn't have committed.

'I will answer their questions truthfully and with brevity and with humility, even though that last thing will come with difficulty. Finn, because I know the truth, and that they are searching for a conviction to adorn their cleverness, they won't see where I will be leading them.'

'Sweet Mother Mary. You are talking the line of an experienced barrister. I can't stop you doing it. My only advice is, you must not show your hand.'

'I will be just like Roadkill with sheep. They won't know it because I will look suitably the slave in this particular master/slave arrangement. At the end they'll be the ones calling "Roro Roro", time to knock off!'

'Jen, I don't want to know your answers. It is enough for me if you are innocent of murder. I believe you. I just hope your self-belief in the truth is enough to dodge the detectives, who have self-belief that they can entrap anybody. My job tomorrow will be to advise you when to say, "No Comment." Do you have anything to ask me?'

'Yes. When can I meet Carmel Blount?'

Finn swallowed hard. They bade each other good night.

In the Lion's Den

A little before ten, Mrs O'Hanlon, flanked by Mr Mahoney, presented herself at the Thredbo Street Police Station in Jindabyne. The weather forecast was for a fine day. That was outside. What would it be on the inside? Finn did the introductions. DI Wilson, DS Merton, this is my client. I don't believe you have met Mrs Jennifer O'Hanlon.

Jen held out her hand, a little limp, unlike her business handshake. She flashed just the briefest smile and its twin, the dimple. There was still another dimple in reserve. Then she lowered her head ever so slightly and put nervous on her face. This was not her natural state of being, not her default mode. It took some acting.

She could have won an Oscar, thought Finn. His admiration went up several notches.

Jen nervously waited to be invited to sit opposite the detectives. She trembled her handbag to the floor. She took in the reactions of the men opposite, man-spreading on their chairs and leaning backwards.

I'll make you lean backwards, thought Jen, but gave nothing away. Gone was yesterday's bossing of Paxton, who was not there to warn the detectives that they were being hunted. And Jen was going to make sure that at the end of however long they took, Wilson and Merton would not know. She hoped that Paxton had not briefed them on the bollocking that he took yesterday. She correctly divined that his male ego would make him keep that to himself.

Wilson, as the senior officer, opened proceedings. Jen knew right then that he was good cop. Wilson politely asked her to state her name out loud for the Nakamichi tape machine before them,

'My name is Mary Flamboya.'

There was a sharp intake of breath of the men present, Finn excluded. He knew, was still unprepared, but not to the extent of sudden urge to breath in like the cops. He thought that that's one to Mary, police zero, even though they were fully acquainted with the name Mary Flamboya.

They did not expect her to come to the lion's den. Please explain was their rather limp opening gambit. Mary showed them her change of name by deed poll.

'You will have to state your name for recording.'

'My name is MARY FLAMBOYA,' rather more loudly than was strictly necessary. Two men opposite flinched involuntarily. Finn admired her delivery from cowering frame. Double Oscar to her!

Next recorded were the names and status of each man present. Wilson addressed the status of Mrs Jennifer O'Hanlon last. When asked to state her occupation, Jen/Mary said, 'I run a coffee shop.'

Wilson stated that Mary was one of scores of people interviewed in relation to crimes committed in Jindabyne. 'Have you associated with any people over this case?'

Finn noticed Wilson's slightly more respectful tone. He caught Mary's eye which narrowed ever so slightly for a millisecond.

Mary replied, 'Yes. Carmel Blount!' before Finn could interject.

Finn groaned inwardly, *What the? She agreed she would not go baiting the detectives.*

Mary just threw a knowing sideways glance at Finn. The detectives thought she was seeking reassurance from her legal advisor at the gaffe she had just made. Finn knew better.

'What was the nature of that association?'

'We were best friends at school and high school. I haven't seen her for more than ten years.'

Mary noticed Wilson relax just a little, but then followed some tension from the seeds of trepidation she had thrown at him. Finn noticed the slight curl of triumph of Jen's lip at the corner, as she threw a nervous glance his way. Talk about wrong-footing Wilson. Carmel had left a lasting wound in his ego. *Jees, she stays on my list of women smarter than myself.*

Merton made nothing of this exchange. The Nakamichi would only have recorded the sort of faux pas that was born of seeming naivety.

Wilson thought, *Have I got another Carmel Blount on my hands?* Full well he remembered his encounter with that formidable woman. It was far too late to coach caution to Merton when their two-faced cop routine came into play.

Finn asked again, 'Could you state for the record exactly what these alleged crimes are? I need to know in order to appropriately advise my client.'

'The suspicious death of Martin O'Hanlon. The postmortem showed he died of strychnine poisoning, administered over an extended period.'

Wilson had hoped that the questioning, at least for a while, could have covered horse theft as well. It might have helped to confuse their obviously nervous interrogee. Win some, lose some. He didn't think that this led to significant loss of advantage.

Mary thought otherwise. She could keep a lot of her powder dry for another interview provided they did not go down that supposed minor path of horse theft. Except that she knew that it was not a minor path, not by a long stretch.

'Your deceased husband was slowly poisoned with strychnine. Did you keep any strychnine in the house?'

'No.'

'Did you have access to strychnine?'

'No.'

'Do you know what strychnine is used for?'

'No.'

'Do you have rat poison in the house?'

'No.'

'Do you know that there is strychnine in rat poison?'

'No.'

'Have you had any experience with rats?'

'Plenty. Four and two-legged. The last ones all male.'

Fragments of uncomfortable smiles, then joke over. Wilson chose to continue his smirk and mirrors style of interrogation, but with a lot less smirk. Finn noticed. He didn't bother a glance to the lip curl from Mary.

'Would you care to explain. You have just told us for the record that there was no rat poison in your house.'

'That is correct. All I know is that when I was young and had a horse at home, the feed shed had rats. You could smell them.'

'What did you do about them?'

'Me. Nothing. My parents would not let me touch the poison that they had. Strictly forbidden. All I know is that they hid it in places that only rats could reach. We had cats and dogs too. Mum and Dad said the poison would kill them if they weren't super careful.'

Merton sensed that Wilson had lost momentum, so took his

bad cop turn. 'You had motive to hate your husband, yes?' said with aggression enough in his voice for the Nakamichi to register.

Mary threw another nervous one at Finn, who nodded. 'I hated him, yes. It was no secret. The whole town knew.'

'It gives you a motive to do him harm, doesn't it?' Merton leaned sharply forward. Mary flinched just enough to convince Merton. Sensing advantage, he pressed on aggressively, 'Enough to kill?'

Finn, 'No comment, Mary. You are not obliged to incriminate yourself.'

'No comment.'

'Let me put it another way. It is a matter of record that you disappeared as soon as the opportunity presented. Was fear of Martin a motive to disappear?'

'Yes.'

'I ask again, did the same motive exist to see him gone?'

'I wished. But there was no way he was going on his own volition.'

'So you admit you had a motive to see him gone, permanently.'

'No comment.'

'You had plenty of opportunity to doctor his food with rat poison, didn't you?'

In spite of Finn's objection, Mary chose to answer. 'If his toast showed the slightest bit of scorch beyond golden yellow, if his coffee wasn't at precisely a poofteenth above just hot, if his eggs were not sunny side up but with not too much runny, he went for me. It beggars belief that you could even think that he wouldn't notice the addition of something foreign into the mix. How would you like to be in my shoes?'

Finn cheered inwardly at Mary's skill in manoeuvring a fulsome reply by disguising an emphatic negative in such a way as not to say no. He admired how she invited a reply of Merton, but who was rendered silent. He wasn't used to having his opinions or feelings tested. He shuffled just the tinsiest little bit, likewise adjusted his forward lean. That was necessary to regain balance, a bit like how a beginner wobbles on a bike.

The bad cop deflated just a little. 'You clearly had the means at hand to poison him, don't you agree?'

Mary cast a nervous glance to her lawyer, but half narrowed her eyes for the regulation millisecond. Finn nodded against his better legal judgment that wanted to say no comment.

'I kept perfect house, just as my husband demanded. He never lifted a finger, but I was houseproud, so I didn't mind. I had mouse traps always set, and a couple of big rat traps that scared me to death. They were sensitive, and the slightest movement would trigger them to go off. And, luckily, they caught maybe only three rodents in ten years. My guess was that the intelligent critters knew there were easier pickings in the stables and feed sheds. I could not touch a dead rat in a trap, with its back broken and bulging eyes and teeth bared.'

She gave a violent shudder. Finn gave an involuntary inner cheer, *That woman, actor extraordinaire, couldn't harm a fly, let alone commit murder.*

Merton had been plainly forced onto the defensive. He stopped his aggressive lean forward. He took a neutral body language stance.

Mary thought to herself, *I told you I would make you lean backward. Next, I'll stop your smug man-spreading; keep your manhood to yourself.*

Wilson took over. 'Did Martin have any enemies?'

'For sure. If he behaved one tenth as badly as he did to me, there would have been stacks. Why do men have to dominate women?'

'Care to give any names?'

'I can't,' she answered truthfully. 'I was as good as in Goulburn Gaol solitary, but with a bit of bail thrown in each week. Like someone had to do the shopping, mugs me, out on parole. You'd know all about that. After years in that place, if you asked an inmate if he had any enemies, they'd as likely say, only the bastard coppers that put me here, the whole lot of you.'

Finn thought of the soccer ref who got tired of being jeered 'who's your father' from the bleachers and demanded an apology from a player who audibly called him a bastard. The player obliged with, 'I'm sorry you're a bastard, ref.'

'Were you aware of any bad things that he may have done?'

'May have! Spare me. Look what he put me through!'

'No, apart from you.'

'You would be better to listen to the rumour mill around Jindy. I couldn't help but overhear gossip. I couldn't wait to escape from it. Martin was timing how long I was away doing the household shopping. I couldn't linger even had I wanted. I have no doubt he had enemies aplenty. What beats me is how he managed to sell horses. Sergeant Paxton would be across all that. Ask him.'

The Nakamichi reel to reel kept spinning, recording Wilson's silence. It's a pity it couldn't record body language. There was plenty of that for posterity to relish, and women's libbers to cheer. Today it would be 'Me too'.

'Did you go to the stables?'

'Only once at the start I did. I married Martin because of horses. I just loved them from when I was a little girl. He pulled on my reins so hard I came to a full halt that would have earned maximum points at dressage. It hurt. He said never to come there again. I could see he meant it. It was too late for me to run. What would you do, DI Wilson?'

Wilson avoided the bait. 'Did you go to the stables again at any time in your ten years of marriage?'

'No.'

'Did you ever notice what was going on down there?'

'Yes. The window behind the kitchen sink points that way. I had plenty of time to see what went on. I spent a lot of time at that sink. Martin saw to that.'

'Like exactly what?'

'Martin trained horses. He had plenty of people who brought problem horses to him. They would stand by the round yard as he disciplined them and trained the owner in what to do.'

'Did you recognise any of his clients?'

'Yes.'

'Names please?'

There was politeness in the air. Straight posture in the chairs. Mary, or Jen as she was back then, rattled off at least ten. They were all young girls. They made up most of the dressage club. Most boys rode up in the mountains. They mocked the one or two boys that rode dressage as 'minced limber in their loafers.'

It was lunch time. Instead of just taking a break, Wilson said, 'Back tomorrow at ten, if it suits you.' Mary had no choice. And Finn was her twin.

'Suits me,' said Mary ever so sweetly. She flashed a more generous helping all round of her smile, and made sure Merton appreciated her dimple.

Once outside, Finn opined, 'That went rather well Jen. Were you happy?'

'Yep. I stopped their smug back-leaning man-spread. Aggressive forward leaning too. Tomorrow they will be like when the teacher calls attention before we marched into school after assembly. Mind you, our best efforts were not in formation like south-flying geese. We were more like the goose gaggle of the barnyard variety. I think Wilson and Merton will do little better.

'Tomorrow, they will question me about horse theft. The day after they will question me about the link between the two. Let's prepare ourselves for rustling, shall we? Shall we rustle up a bit of lunch?'

'It's on me,' said Finn. 'What about we unmuzzle ourselves for a very late counter lunch at the pub? I won't bill you for it. I think I understand the economics of that. I would like to get a feeling for the locals. See if it might help our cause.'

Finn could not mask his utter amazement at the scene within. Jen had expected it, that cantina scene from *Star Wars*, still six years hence. A wretched hive of scum and villainy on the surface, fine folk underneath, Jen knew.

It was payday. It was dole day. The hippies came out of their home-made eco houses, the hermit from his hovel. The rouseabouts, ringers, and stockmen came down from the hills with their paycheques, denim work gear clad, RM Williams boots, horseman high-heeled. The pub acted as banker, because that way the publican could get a share of the paycheques. Each fortnight he organised an Armaguard van to deliver the cash.

Driver and offsider wore sidearms to deter the modern bushranger. They were, police apart, the only civilians authorised to carry guns. They had a third khaki uniform sat in the back with a shotgun, double barrel.

Cash did not pass over the public bar, the private bar, or the lounge, where the women were supposed to be. Women's libbers were to put paid to that before much longer.

There was a room out the back, that served for the exchange of cheque for cash. There was trust based on long-standing custom. The only precaution taken was to make sure the cheques were endorsed by the payee.

No mark, no Moola, thought Finnbar, smiling at his own hometown pun.

Two sidearms-packing men in khaki acted as guarantor. No drunkenness was allowed in the exchange room. None was possible because the payees had no cash before the cash from the cheque. That's why the process started at four on the dot and went on for as many hours as it took. The nearby were there soon after knockoff. Others drifted in in order of distance travelled. Their wives and girlfriends came as drivers, necessary after the swill. They had further to drive the latecomers who came from farther away.

Their dress defied description as far as Finnbar was concerned. Many had denim held up with a piece of twine. Most had on a stockman's belt, with horseshoe brass buckle, ring, and pouch for pocketknife. Another bigger knife in a sheath of the belt. It was legal for them because they were standard work gear. If they came across stock with a broken leg, they humanely slit its throat. Butchered the carcass later.

The shearers among that flock wore jackie howes, those blue singlets that exposed shoulders and arms muscled by heavy sheep. No gym work required here on triceps and biceps. They were steeped in lanoline and sheep smell.

The ringer had de rigueur RM Williams heavy cotton checked shirt, with baccy and paper for their roll-yer-owns stashed in each pocket. In cool weather they wore a vest over. More pockets full of stash. In winter, it was a heavy sheepskin coat, pockets full of hands. The hats were western style leather. Battered. Or Akubra rabbit fur felt, western, battered. Did new hats ever exist in the Snowy country? The style of each denoted rank. No squatter hats here.

It was the hippies that really amazed Finnbar. They adorned with bandannas, scarves, jewellery even on the men, necklaces and bracelets by the dozen and made of leather, hemp, or straw. They could be beaded – donkey beads were particularly popular – or wrapped in fabric. Some men wore flowing gowns, multi-coloured, tie died. They smelled of mind-altering substances, soon to be indistinguishable from the rancid smell of breath expelled over beer glass foam.

And the ferals! – never washed, never shaved, never a haircut. Stunk.

Jen smiled at his surprise. Finn was amazed beyond whistle. He did wet his whistle though on a schooner of Reschs – 'Wretches' to other states' drinkers. Mary stuck to a pony of shandy. She didn't much like beer.

On the way out, Mary noticed a big man with a bushy flaming red Ned Kelly beard. There was something vaguely familiar about him. He would look like granite on a horse. Finn asked what was she uneasy about. She didn't answer because she didn't really know herself. She just hoped the big man hadn't noticed her.

Encore

Once home, they freshened up, Jen first in the only bathroom. Deliciously showered, she used the squeegee to wipe down the glass screens, as though she were horse caring. She hung her wet towel on the middle of the towel ladder, top rung left vacant for Finn. She pulled out, just so, another guest towel. Not even a man could miss the intent.

She wrapped her wet hair in a third towel, piled high on her head, securely tucked into itself. A turban. She put on comfortable lounge-about clothes for the evening's work. That top hat would come off when it had done its absorbent duty.

She hummed as she called out to Finn, 'Your turn.' Finn was a bit surprised in the transformation, fresh smelling, mood likewise, crumple-free loose smock, sheepskin Uggboot slippers, a hint of scent, and the ballet dance step on the way to 'her' chair. Just a speck of toothpaste on her chin. Like a beauty spot that is the flaw that enhances pure beauty.

Finn thought, *Blind Martin. Didn't he see the treasure that he had?*

Then he couldn't help but think, *How did I get to here, rolling down winding way?*

He too emerged clean and uncrumpled, teeth brushed, throat gargled, glass of water drunk, ready for more preparatory work. No toothpaste dribble.

Jen said, 'We've only just eaten. I'll knock up supper when we get peckish.'

On each side table, there was a glass of favourite tipple. This time, for Martin, there was an ice bucket with tongs hanging on the side, next to a Waterford crystal tumbler part-filled with a precise measure of Ireland's finest.

On her own fine delicate bone china entrée plate there were slices of lemon, plus one already draped on her high ball glass of gin and tonic, this time with one big lump of ice. Tiny silver tongs completed that ensemble. Clearly their quota tonight was to be more than one. Two bottles stood abreast on the drinks sideboard. Break a leg.

After glass clink up high for libation, glasses descended for polite sip and lip smack. Jen opened up first. After all, she had the information, Finn being there just for finer points of law.

Jen started, 'You noticed I was uneasy over something as we left the pub. I still am but I don't know what for. It might come to me as we talk about horse rustling. You are wondering how I am so certain that tomorrow's grilling will be about missing nags.

'They had wanted to talk about them today. You cut them short at the pass. Thank you. It was and will be easier tackling that duo one subject at a time. You will agree that we came out with a handy lead. They will sit politely tomorrow, so I won't have to apply another half-halt on their reins.'

Finn puzzled why Jen thought tomorrow would be all about horse theft.

'They didn't get much change out of me about murder, murder by me that is. Even though they now think it less likely that I was the poisoner. Don't you agree? Unlikely but not unreasonable to think that I might be. They would be talking right now about how to handle me.

'And they would be licking their wounds after failing the grade so far. They are not stupid. They are experienced after all. They are bound to come at it from another angle. And that angle has to be horse theft. Someone clever has to be behind that. I am in a position to know something about that. Probably the only person apart from the thief or thieves.

'They still think I know something, more than they have gleaned so far. Because you got the interviewers to cover only poisoning, I could altogether avoid horse talk. Thank you again. You don't know how important that is.'

Finn nodded his admiration for her intuitive thinking, her seeing through the would-be entrappers. He still couldn't see it. He knew her well enough by now to know that she would tell in her own good time, and then the logic would be plain for him to see. He elevated Jen to co-equal with Carmel in the list of women cleverer than him. You can't get a higher mark than high distinction at law school. That is, unless you get dux and gold medal at the end.

Jen, in Finn's eyes, had just scored dux and gold medal in the school of hard knocks.

'Now, as I told the cops, I spent a lot of time at the kitchen sink. I implied it was because I was so busy pandering to Martin's every whim and demand. There was more to it than that. I was spying.'

Finn gave an involuntary start. Jen noticed.

'There were lots of comings and goings that helped me with coping. There was nothing in it for a long time. Just watching life in action, life that I could not share in. It made me sad in that way. It kept me occupied in another, by forcing me to play a sort of game.

'That game gradually took on a life of its own. Over time I started to make mental notes of how many times individuals would be down there with Martin. You'd be surprised how I soon had a picture of who to expect on what days, what they came for, who for riding lessons, who for horse behaviour training, who for the selling or the buying of horses.

'Dressage lessons? Almost all young girls. Some I knew by name, but as time went by, fewer and fewer. I just remembered them by how they arrived, the sort of horse float, whether or not they drove themselves, that sort of thing. I envied them. They should have been me.

'Horse obedience saw a lot more young men, but still quite a lot of young women. They had usually become proficient riders, but had probably gone out and bought a new horse, which turned out to have things that needed sorting out. Martin was very good at that sort of thing. A real horse whisperer.

'The young men usually wanted their stock horses trained up super fast. Martin knew all the tricks and was happy to oblige. Word of mouth was his best advertisement.

'Finally there were horses that came and went. Martin was buying and selling, some newly caught brumbies from the mountains. They might come in singly or small groups. Then I would see a big horse transporter come in, or it might be Martin's own big truck.'

'Where is this leading, Jen? I don't want to stop you, because it is interesting to me. But what was unusual?'

'Well, it took a long time for me to cotton on. You see, there was always a vehicle per horse, and sometimes two people per car. Mum might be the chauffer for example. Or a proud dad might come along to watch. That's what this dressage game is like.

'Then when horses were taken out in Martin's big truck, he always needed a helper with the loading. It was possible to do it with just one man, but a lot slower.

'The penny dropped one day – how did Martin's helper get there? No extra vehicle ever arrived. You can imagine how I relished this challenge to keep me occupied. I wished I could have been that helper. With bastard Martin, no way.

'Until that revelation, I had never kept count of people and horses at any one time. Then I started to make it my business, by hook or by crook. It was memory training, I can tell you. I had to remember lots of shapes and sizes, how they walked, whatever identified the person. I was, let's admit it, spying. It was not stalking, before I never wanted and there never was going to be any chance of meeting up with them in real life.

'I had to match a person with a horse. Not hard, I found out, because horse and rider in dressage went together, and owner and horse being disciplined in the round yard were always together. The unknown was the horse being bought or sold, when the horse and owner had no reason to spend much time together.

'Bear with me, Finn, we are nearly there. A horse without an owner, now that's completely understandable. Tell me, Finn, what would you think about a person without a horse? That person was a man by the way.'

'I'd wonder what was the person there for. What sort of vehicle?'

'Exactly for point one. Point two, the man did not have a vehicle!'

Finn's senses picked up. 'No wonder you grew curioser and curioser. I would too. Did you come to any conclusions?'

'No. I still can't.'

'What did he look like?

'He was a very big man. I think I know who he is. And I bet the cops don't.'

The Big Man

Jen and Finn entered the bar. They were instantly noticed. Especially on this payday. Strangers had that habit of attracting such attention. No mystery why. There was no reason why a tourist would come here on this day of days.

A big man with a flaming red beard down to this waist entered the hotel a long way down the field. He lived and worked a fair way away, but there were many more remote than him that used the pub as a bank. They'd pack down in that unseemly scrum in their own good time. Each new man would be greeted with 'Owyergoinmateorright'. No one ever shook hands.

Naturally the well-dressed duo struck the big man instantly. It's like a stranger wandering into the cow bails at milking time. Every cow will turn its loosely secured head around to look. They sense via smell and sight that a newcomer is in their midst. Then they look at you so slowly with such kindly eyes. And so it is with a country pub, especially on payday. Why else would you come here? A stranger must have a special reason.

The big man took in the bar scene. It did not strike him as stare-worthy like it did for strangers. Like it did for Finn. He was only glance-worthy to the big man. The attractive woman with him was more than that. He looked long and hard, but nothing much registered. A little bit did though. His look was not cow-eye slow and kindly. His eyes were startling green for one thing, and rather small for that big, red-encircled head.

When she left an hour or so later, that little bit no longer registered. There was foam on the whiskers spilling over the borders of his mouth. There was foam on his sleeve from periodic wiping the foam away to give freer entry of the beer from the glass.

He did not notice the slightly troubled glance from the beautiful one as she exited close by Red Ned. Only Finn noticed her unease. By then she had been sipping on her pony for nearly an hour. The big man had quaffed three schooners. He was in the process of talking garble like all the other men in the bar. It grew noisier by the minute. The proprietor was in the process of profiting from his unofficial banking business, by the minute.

For the big man the night was but a pup. The next morning would be a fair bitch. He would wake up with a head far bigger than usual. The length of his memory would not match the size of his head. But he would remember the beautiful one.

Back in the Lion's Den

Next morning Jen and Finn descended the steep hill behind the Jindabyne shopping centre, from their house overlooking the lake, on their way to Thredbo Street. Part way along, Jen said, 'Want to have a bet? Just for fun. No money.'

'Okay. Just for fun. I wouldn't bet money against you if my life depended on it.'

'Well spoken, like a true loser,' said Jen. 'Soon I'm going to be Mary again. That actually fits my head better, to tell you the truth. I've been Mary since I shot through.' She carefully didn't say which Mary. Chiaprisi was her own private surprise. 'We are going to play a quick game of rock, paper, scissors.'

They stood just so, fists beyond bump as the action began. One, two, three, show!

Mary showed one finger. Finn showed two. 'Finn you win. Scissors beat paper. You name one cop we front inside.'

'Wilson.'

Shake shake shake flash. Jen flashed three, Finn his regulation two. Rock beats scissors. 'Paxton!'

'Jesus wept, Mary. Where did that come from?'

'We have to have a deal breaker. One more try. We can't go in there one apiece.'

Shake shake shake flash. The lady flashed one finger, the man three. Rock beats paper. 'Merton.'

'Okay,' said Mary. 'You win this bit of fun two to one. I bet you that you are wrong when we see the finish of the horse race inside.'

'Jees, Mary, I can't win against you even when I win,' said Finn. 'Water beats everything. I say it's going to be the same as yesterday – Wilson and Merton. Good cop and bad cop. That team wants to make amends for yesterday.'

'Wilson and Paxton.'

'You're on. Winner buys lunch. Bless Blarney, and the Pope too, I hope there's enough money in my purse.'

They both laughed a joyful laugh, which was to be their last for quite a few hours. Finn's face held station, the same look as usual until his Irish eyes lit up at some witticism or other, usually emanating from his mouth.

Mary's smile evaporated into the ether, her dimple like the last of the Cheshire cat's smile in Alice's wonderland. She lowered her head just a tad, a wee bit hesitant, and they walked into the police station.

In the interview, they sat down in the same places as yesterday. Isn't it funny how quickly habits form? A young constable offered them coffee. Mary said her usual, 'Hope it's good coffee,' then accepted their instant swill with all the good grace she could muster.

In walked Wilson and sat where yesterday. What's that about habits again? The tension in the air was palpable. After what seemed an eternity to Finn, who was holding his breath, in came ... Mary correctly surmised that this delay was a Wilson tactic to throw Mary off balance, just a wee bit, but off balance nonetheless. Finn would have seen it many times in his career. The New York brat John McEnroe was to perfect the tactic at tennis, in between tantrums.

In walked Paxton, not very convincingly uttering apologies.

'Sorry I'm late.'

Mary cast a sly sideways at Finn, who pretended not to notice, even though he had. She noticed that particular Finn's 'not noticed'. She smiled inwardly. There was a bet to be collected – the most expensive meal that Jindabyne had to offer. Finn had done well to wonder if there was enough money in his purse.

'Just as well I didn't bet my life on it.' All the same, Finn thought that he had never had this much fun at work before in his unbettable life.

Paxton turned on the Nakamichi reel to reel, the finest tape recorder that Japan could produce.

'The time is ten a.m. on Tuesday 13 March 1971. I am Detective Inspector Wilson of the Sydney Criminal Investigation Branch.

'I am Sergeant Paxton of the Jindabyne Police.'

'I am Finnbar Mahoney of Mahoney & Geeves, Moola Moola, New South Wales. I am legal advisor to Mary Flamboya.' A slightly surprised look flashed over Paxton, even though he had been forewarned.

'I am Mary Flamboya of 51 Ocean Street Subiaco, Perth, Western Australia. I run a coffee shop.'

Wilson led. No surprise there. Master before minion. 'Today should be quicker than yesterday. We will talk only about horse rustling; that's why Sergeant Paxton is here. He has been the lead man-on-the-spot all along, so he knows all the ins and outs.'

Mary had the night before resolved not to repeat her two days ago mauling of Sergeant Paxton. But, never let a chance go by. She felt like saying, 'Then why was it Sydney Flying Squad placed that ad in *The West Australian*? About horse rustling becoming a serious business in the Monaro. Why not placed by the Snowy Mountains police?'

Mary thought and thought and thought these thoughts, but she never said them. She was thinking about ocean lobster and mountain trout lunch. And smiling at the thought that Finn would have pronounced it 'taught' – no wasted h's in his talk.

Formalities over, the cops cut straight to the chase. Wilson, 'Tell us who you think is the horse rustler?'

Who needs bad cop? thought Mary.

'Mary, you don't have to speculate if you don't know.'

Mary, 'I don't know.' Even though she was pretty sure about it. She wanted to be absolutely sure before offering an official opinion. Not a public one either for the matter.

'You have told the police that you were certain your husband was not a horse thief.'

'I don't remember that.'

'It's on the record. Your interview two days ago with Sergeant Paxton.'

'Sorry. I do remember now. I'd forget my head if it wasn't screwed on.'

'Okay. How did you know that Martin O'Hanlon was innocent?'

'This could take a little time.'

'Take all the time you need.'

'Well, it's like this. At his trial, the police didn't want me as a witness. It could have been sorted out there and then. I guess the police were thinking, what would a mere female know about strictly men's business.'

Finn groaned to himself. *Mary promised not to give the police another bollocking.*

'I wasn't so sure of my facts at the time of the trial anyway. With the benefit of hindsight, I am now. Actually, I was very soon afterwards as a matter of fact. Twenty twenty vision and all that. But by then it was too late. I went through all the paperwork as soon as I had the house to myself, just to make sure. As soon as Martin had free board at the Cooma lockup.

'That bookwork was always in good shape. It was my responsibility. Martin double-checked everything'—Mary resisted saying 'everyting'—'and all the filing too.

'I started with invoices and receipts, looking at only the ones to do with the buy and sell of horses. I wasn't interested in the receipts from the supermarket for household shopping. I already knew those dollars and cents backwards. Why bastard Martin wanted all that filed was beyond me. If I wanted to stash away a little money for myself from the household budget, believe me Martin would never have known how I did it. But I didn't. How could I spend such money without Martin noticing I had one too many haircuts this half year? Forget about pleading for colour streaks. And what could I do with nice shoes?

'I looked through the records of every horse sold, finishing with the invoice for the selling commission. Martin did most of this on consignment, but a lot he had bought or caught and trained up. I matched every receipt for horse bought with its receipt from the Cooma Saleyards. I ticked off those he had caught against the branding book entry. And this all for the last twelve months. Everything matched. Well, almost.'

Paxton, 'How did you know that the horse sold was the same as horse bought?'

'I have a memory for horses. Have done all my life. And for good horses, the sires and dams going back to way back when. Blood lines are everyting. Ever bet on the Melbourne Cup?'

There goes that baiting again, thought Finn.

'Every horse had to have a delivery chit. That way the saleyards confirmed the number of horses on offer. No room for slipping in an extra. They kept the original. The driver kept the duplicate. I reckon only Martin kept the duplicates on file. They are the sort of thing that even the taxman doing an audit on you would not ask for. And they want to know what you have for breakfast.

'You can see that I did an audit just as tough as the taxman. No doubt about it. Martin had stolen no horse. Someone had come to him with falsified paperwork. If the police had done their work carefully, they would not even have taken Martin to court. And don't expect me to have gone to the police with what I knew. By then I had done ten years in my own private gaol, courtesy of my husband. Talk about for better or for worse, till death do us part. So all I wanted was for bastard Martin to taste a little of what it was like. He would get only four months with good behaviour. I had done ten years. Spare me. Or I'll go spare.'

Mary cowered a little as she spat out these words. Just for emphasis. As if her words needed it. Wilson did not want to pursue that line of questioning any further. He knew that Mary had him by the short and curlies. And not just the ones on the back of his neck.

'I'm sorry that the police have let you down. There is an inquiry going on as we speak. You won't have to appear before it. The transcript from this interview will suffice.

'Before I hand over to Sergeant Paxton, just one more question from me for now. The court records show that six horses from a remote station were sold without the owner's knowledge. They also show that Martin O'Hanlon's truck was the transporter, driven by Adam Yates, better known as Bumfluff. Most people didn't even know his real name. They also show Martin as the "owner" of the horses. With the benefit of hindsight and your careful audit, how was all that possible?'

'Here's what I think. I don't know for sure, but I want to help you all I can to find the real culprits.'

Polish your halo some more, thought Finn. Softly softly catchee monkey.

'I have just told you that all the paperwork was in order, well almost. That "almost" is important. It does not mean that it was my mistake. The fact is, no money was banked into Martin's account from that sale of six horses.

'I know that sounds impossible. It took me a while to figure it out. How how how? I doubt the police have to this day'—there goes that baiting again, delivered with downcast eyes—'In fact, I think I am the only person in the world that could figure it out.'

Total surprise registered on Finn's face. Coppers too. How could this mild mannered one claim smarts over all of manhood?

'It must have taken real cunning to have Bumfluff as the delivery driver that day. I reckon that cunning one also went to the sales that day. After the sale, that person went up to Bumfluff, and handed him a piece of paper, in an envelope, and said to hand over the "cheque" in the Cooma Saleyards envelope to Martin for banking. Bumfluff could hardly read or write, so he did as he was asked.

'Bumfluff must have been known to that person, or he wouldn't have handed over the "cheque" to him. Cheques were made out usually to "XXXX YYYY or Bearer". The saleyards folk knew the flexibility that this afforded was necessary in the way that business is done in the bush. Cheques have to be cashable at the pub. Now comes the part that explains why I was and am the only one capable of solving this mystery. Anybody here got a clue?' Bait bait.

Desperate as the cops were, Finnbar for the matter too, they could only shake their heads in resignation.

Mary allowed herself only the fleetest of triumph. 'Bumfluff delivered to Martin what he thought was a cheque to him, payable bearer, in a Cooma Saleyards envelope. He didn't bother to check its contents, as per usual. He asked Bumfluff to take it up to me to put it into the satchel for later banking.

'Still no idea boys?' Bait bait.

The 'boys' all wished the teasing would come to an end soon.

Finn was the only 'boy' that thought he had never had so much fun at work before. After a longish pause for dramatic effect came the revelation.

'Inside that envelope was only a cooking recipe! For a moment I chose to think that I had a newfound cooking friend somewhere. A few seconds later I knew that Martin had been scammed. I did not know who by. Martin always did the banking himself. Bastard. So I had to make sure he did not bank the cooking recipe. He would not have known that the expected cheque for those horses had disappeared.'

All male eyes around that table rounded in surprise at how Mary had probably exposed the fraud. So simple that nobody had thought of it. The Nakamichi recorded quite a bit of silence. The cops did not want to have recorded that which confirmed how ham-fisted had been the investigation, how feeble the prosecution case, how wrong the verdict.

The transcript would go to the inquiry. Let them fix it up. Somebody would sue the police no doubt. And they were worried the litigant was sitting opposite them. Mary read their thoughts and luxuriated in how she had again managed things to her advantage. Finn didn't need telling. That wordless communication, the slit-eyed sideways glance, this time held for long enough for the tormentors opposite to notice, was quite enough.

'*Assuming* ...'—lamely emphasising that word—'*assuming* that is a correct version of events, does that leave us with Tom Dooley, in spite of all his protestations to the contrary, and TwoBoots, as the chief suspects?' said Paxton placing his Hercule Poirot qualifications on parade.

'Maybe,' was all that Mary delivered with a hopeless shrug of her shoulders.

Exit Paxton stage left, thought Finn. Mary had totally blocked exit right.

Wilson, 'When was the last time you saw Tom Dooley?'

'1968.'

'Care to elaborate?'

'Nothing to elaborate. It was the year before Martin was being questioned.'

'When did you last talk to Tom Dooley?'

'When we were in first year at high school. I wiped him like a dirty rag when Eva Rumford told me what handsome charming Tom was really like. Bastard.'

'What's your favourite word?'

'Bastard. But only when it is literally correct.'

Wilson's attempt at joke and levity had fallen flat on his face. He persisted, as any interrogator would, knowing it would pay off in the long run, however long that might be. 'Would you say that Tom is an habitual criminal?'

'Yes. Tom moves from town to town when people noticed that things go missing when he is around. You already know that, I presume.'

Paxton, Wilson and Co never confirmed anything that they may have learned during interrogations. 'Would you say that he could graduate to serious crime?'

'I'm no criminologist. He could, but he needn't. He needs serious help before he keeps on the path that he doesn't seem to be able to get off. Maybe the police could arrange for sessions with a criminal psychologist?'

Paxton wasn't going there. 'Are you going to talk to Tom now you are back in town?'

'Hell no. He is still a toe rag to me.'

'When was the last time you talked to Freddy Ford, aka TwoBoots?'

Paxton had read MS Merton's record of interview with Eva Britten and was interested to compare her opinion with Mary's. Oh! And to trap her into saying something inconsistent, a fib perhaps, or something deliberate to mislead. Mary knew that he would have read it, but of course never let on. Her intuition was her business, until she chose to use it.

'At high school.'

'Did you have much contact?'

'Quite a bit. Freddy Ford was a likeable boy, a big lad. He was a star footballer, so we all spoke with him quite a bit.'

'Was there anything about him that stood out apart from football?'

'He had feet of two different sizes. You would know that's how come his nickname. TwoBoots copped that from all sides. Cooma cheer squad cheering and opponents snarling "TwoBoots" at him. I know he hurt. Didn't show it. He was secretive, hid things from others, looked guilty a lot but what for I don't know. He was hard to read. He was a hard box to open.'

'Now where have I heard that description before?' mused the Sergeant. 'Have you been talking to Eva Britten about TwoBoots?'

'Who's Eva Britten?'

'Don't tell me you don't know! She was a Rumford before she married BB.'

'Oh, that Eva. Yes, we were good mates at school and high school. I lost touch when I married Martin. The bastard.'

'Did you talk to Eva Rumford-Britten about TwoBoots?'

'I refer to my previous reply. The only person I have talked to since I came back is my legal advisor. But now that you mention it, where does Eva live?'

'Boolaba, out west.'

It was Mary's turn to be surprised, but she wasn't going to

explain it to Paxton. Finn already knew.

'Are there any other former classmates we should talk to?'

'Well, yes,' thought Mary. 'But at this stage you're not going to hear it from me.'

'Then tomorrow at ten sharp again,' came the full stop from Wilson.

As they left, Finn commented, 'These interviews were being dragged out by the police. Probably deliberately.'

Mary just smiled, 'All the more free feeds on you.'

Two Boots

Good to her betting word, Mary took them to a fish and chips place. Having lost his ill-advised wager to her, Finn liked the idea of forking out only for a feed wrapped in paper. *Some for the beggar seagulls*, he thought, as he saw themselves sitting and dining al fresco on the bench by the lake. And then out loud, 'I wonder why they aren't called lakegulls?'

She smiled her full repertoire, and that dimple never dug so deep. She gave Finn the full geography of her voice. 'Why do you always speak Irish? There's sit down out the back,' accurately reading the lawyer's thought.

'Taught' to Finn, she chuckled to herself. *I'll teach him!*

They went 'out the back'. It was anything but flash, but Mary preferred good food to silver service any day. The plastic cloths over Formica tables with chrome bent pipe legs gave Finn even more comfort. Short lived.

They sat down. He took a double turn when Mary ordered lobster mornay for starters, mountain trout on a bed of wild black rice for main, accompanied by a stack of organic vegetables. Oh, and just one glass of your best white. Himself can do without. He resigned himself, shook his head left to right and back again ever so slowly, and asked himself, *Why am I not surprised?*

Finn emitted a groan, passed on the mornay, but ordered the same trout as Mary. 'Win none, lose the lot', he complained out loud. In the next breath he told Mary that he had never had more fun at work. Luckily the bank was next door.

Mary shared her mornay. 'It's too much for one anyway. And women have smaller appetites than men,' escaped from Mary's half full mouth. 'Especially men as big as you, Finn.'

'Now you tell me,' mock-grumbled Finn, with a smile. They lingered over lunch, small talk only. Their evening session would see serious planning for the morrow.

Once home, the yesterday's preparations were repeated. With two big differences. One, Mary emerged her usual fresh, but no towel turban on her head this time. Inside the bathroom she had hung a wet shower cap hung up on a hook. It had 'Forza' stylishly rendered alongside a stylised coffee bean on the front at a jaunty angle.

Two, she had a completely different fashion, a designer track suit that looked nothing like the ones out of Kmart. Subiaco cool.

Finn emerged dressed in his same old same old. He wryly observed that he needed fashionista advice and badly.

They clinked glasses, the short and the tall, one lemon shod, the both of them with mini-icebergs, same as yesterday. Mary opened proceedings. Finn noticed the two bottles out on the ready. The thought made him relish the coming repeats.

'The cops think that there are two persons of interest left to discuss. So do I, except my quinella is not the same as theirs. They reckon first Tom Dooley, second TwoBoots. I reckon first TwoBoots, second someone else. Tom will be there as a total decoy.'

'I won't bet, but methinks your second is the big man.'

'Right on. Pity you didn't put any money on it.'

'No worries. Win none, lose none.'

Mary said, 'There's nothing much we can prepare for the interrogation about Tom Dooley. Minor bastard. Hardly worth the word. His petty criminal history is there for all to see. I think he is just too petty to be involved in poisoning. Forging horse papers is above his pay grade too I reckon. He's more the shoplifter type. What do you think?'

'Agreed. You'll just have to wing it. They can't extract blood from a stone. You have already explained that you girls all dropped him like a hot potato at age fifteen or so. That leaves TwoBoots as their real target in tomorrow's interview. Now, we don't know what Paxton and co have on TwoBoots. I reckon they must have something important, or they wouldn't be bothering us for a t'ird day.

'For once, Mary, I have more information than you. Or at least I know how to get more on TwoBoots.'

Mary was not in the least bothered, and said so. 'I am paying you good money to be my legal advisor. The more you earn your keep, the happier me. Pray tell.'

'A while ago DS Jack Merton interviewed the Brittens in Boolaba. Wilson his self did ditto with Carmel Blount. Naturally Carmel has kept me across the details. I have not spoken to Eva since. With your agreement, I will ring her now to ask about it.' The 'his self' was not lost on Mary.

'Cool. Could you do it over speaker phone so we both can talk and listen?'

'Why not. Just make sure that it doesn't become a reunion. Ten minutes. I don't want to be up all night.'

He dialled Eva in Boolaba. Mary wondered how come the number was in his head. Finn soon had her agreement. They had hit it off from the first, at the Moola Club, and besides, it would be so good for her to talk to Jen O'Hanlon after so long. Finn said that Jen was now Mary Flamboya. That bought a surprised reaction from Eva, 'How very Jen to choose such a stylish name!'

Finn gave a broad outline of how the detectives Wilson and

Merton, and Sergeant Paxton of the Jindabyne police, had been interviewing Mary over the course of a few days. Naturally he didn't give anything away, and Eva understood without having it spelled out in big capital letters.

'Tomorrow the talk will be all about TwoBoots. What can you tell me that Merton may have learned about him from you?'

'No worries. I can summarise what I told him, because it was obvious he was fishing for anything, anything at all because clearly they had nothing at that stage. I told Merton how the nickname came about, how TwoBoots was popular and a great footballer, how he had moved to Merimbula, how I had heard he was doing well there. I also told him that he always seemed to be hiding something, or at least keeping something to himself. I said, that in a word, he was secretive.

'That might help you for tomorrow. Knowing Merton, he will ask all those sorts of innocuous questions, so just answer as you see fit. Now there's one thing I reckon is important, and you had better discuss this between yourselves as to how you handle it.'

Finn knew he was held in the thrall of these two smart women. Just as well Carmel wasn't on this party line as well. 'Fire away.'

'TwoBoots was in Jindabyne each month visiting his mum and dad. I saw him there because his mum lived a few doors from mine. A couple of hours drive, give or take. Pity help you in winter with fog on Brown Mountain.

'I teased Merton a bit about guessing the days of his visit. For sure he failed that test I set him. But his ears pricked up when I said it was always on a Thursday, and not just any Thursday. It was sales day at the Cooma stockyards!' Finn whistled a half bar of something Irish.

'Eva, I can't thank you enough. No wonder the police have him in their pocketbooks as a person of interest! Now I'll leave you to natter to Mary for a while. When we get back, we must all go to the Club. Celebrate or commiserate, doesn't matter which.'

The natter lasted ten minutes. Precisely.

Mary said, 'Finn, that information is worth at least a Sweet Jesus. Now, I'm no sayer of sooth, but clearly our secretive hero TwoBoots has something to hide, and for sure Wilson will pump me for all it's worth just to see if I know.'

'Do you know, Mary? This could hold a key to a lot of tings.'

'I do, as a matter of fact. I didn't stand at that kitchen sink staring down towards the lower forty for nothing. Remember our first night's debriefing? I told you there often seemed to be a spare man. Spare in the sense that he didn't come by car, of that I'm sure.

'Remember also that I did not tell this to the cops at our interview that first day, nor today. Now, the distance down to where Martin did his work was quite a way away. Too far to recognise faces. That's why I used size if it was unusual. Gait from my dressage days was just as important in people as horses.'

Finn interrupted, eager to put his cleverness on display, 'So you could've picked out TwoBoots by his gait?'

'My you are a clever one. That's right. Now that I think of it, TwoBoots was like a metronome. Every second Thursday in the month, he rocked up. And rocked around, ha ha. I would never have come to this realisation if it was not for Eva.

'Now, is it possible that TwoBoots and the big man always came together to Martin's on sale day? You know, like Laurel and Hardy, Tom and Jerry, black and white, fish and chips?'

'Do you have to remind me how much lunch cost me today?'

'Nice lunch it was too. Now, is it possible that big man and TwoBoots came in the same car or ute? That would explain why I often thought that there was one man left over.'

Over two slow tipples off the top shelf, they prodded this information left and right, up and down, inside out and all over the place. They could not prod it to any reasonable station.

The prodding exposed half a dozen possibilities, from the logical through the ridiculous to the cor blimey. They finished the evening with a few savoury party pies, cleaned their teeth, and good nighted each other, well prepared as could be for what was to come next day at ten on the dot.

Mary was emphatic that there should be no talk of the big man. That would have to wait for another day, when they had developed the case against big man a lot further. When they presented that to the detectives, even Finn was certain that they would not have to come to Jindabyne again. The cops would come to them in Moola Moola, try to stop them!

The Awakening

'Oozing charm from every pore
He oiled his way around the floor'

My Fair Lady

Bob Paxton was a smart plod. He learned quickly from the bollocking that Mary had delivered him that first time at the police station. He learned from the master class delivered to himself and Wilson by the aptly named Ms Flamboya. He was ambitious and liked to make every post a winner. He was very young to be in charge of a station. Here was his chance to impress in a mystifying case not too many young cops had had to face in their young working lives. He would work the lower part of his anatomy off to make sure of it. If any clue was left lying around, he would hit it for six.

He re-read the second forensic report that he himself had initiated. No surprise when Wilson had authorised it, hang the expense.

Wilson read the same report, preparing for day three interview. Merton had returned to Sydney. Paxton would have inside running tomorrow. It was he who had uncovered this new and critical information. This young man had formulated a reasonable synthesis of what had really happened at the O'Hanlon ranch. He had shifted the action from the house to the stables and sheds, where the poisoning must have occurred. The rustling hardly took place in the house. And it seemed clear that that crime had been planned elsewhere.

Jennifer O'Hanlon aka Mary Flamboya held vital information on both crimes, of that they were both now convinced. Tomorrow would help clear up the mystery. Bring it on.

Next day everyone sat in their usual place, like a dog does. The only difference, Mary thought, was that these people didn't spin twice before sitting down. Wilson opened proceedings with polite small talk. Hope you had a nice evening and all that sort of stuff. Too polite. Mary braced herself. She didn't much like this turn of the detective.

Finn was relaxed. He really didn't have to do anything that he hadn't done a hundred times before. 'I'll hand over to Sergeant Paxton.'

'Who did Tom Dooley mix with most at high school?'

'Not with me. Not with my friends. He was a dirty toe rag to us.'

'I know that. Who were his friends after that?'

'Lots of other boys. No girls. That Tom was a charmer, and boys are not as mature as girls. They can't see through things like us girls.'

Bait bait bait, thought Finn. She can't help herself. She no doubt felt confident that he, Finn, could see. Not that he had been granted a dispensation from mere malehood. No. She knew Paxton had his left brain focussed on the interview. No way of engaging the right side at the same time. Not like us girls. Suck it up, men.

'What was the chatter about Tom?'

'Keep clear of light fingers. He can't help his thieving ways.'

'Did any boy stand out as closest to Tom?'

Mary saw where this was leading. Finn too, but a minute later.

'Well yes. There was one. His name was Eddie Murray. That was only for first year. He moved with his family to somewhere in the Illawarra or Southern Highlands, I think. I never saw him again.' She wasn't sure that last bit was totally true. There was no present truth that she could give them though.

'Did Tom Dooley see Martin when you became Mrs O'Hanlon?'

'Yes. He was there often. I asked Martin about "Toe Rag" as I called him. Martin went off his face. We never discussed it again.'

'What did you think Toe Rag was doing there?'

'Nothing good, that's for sure.'

'So he could have been plotting a horse scam with Martin?'

'That thought never entered my head. Well, maybe just a bit. Tom might have been manipulating Martin into selling dodgy horses.'

'How so?'

'Horses with dodgy brands. Martin probably didn't dig too deep so long as the altered brand would pass muster on sale day.'

'Did you notice any "dodgy" money in the banking?'

'No. By then everything would have been made legit.'

'Well, how did Tom benefit?'

'I noticed early on that Tom drew wages from Martin. Now, that raised my suspicions. But nobody else would ever notice. If they did, Martin could legitimately say that Tom was poisoning weeds. Paterson's curse was a problem. Skeleton weed had to be pulled out by the roots. No known chemical treatment. Bastard of a job. Tom would never do an honest day's work in his life.'

'So Martin was guilty of something in your eyes?'

'Yes.'

'That's enough on Tom. You've been most helpful.'

Mary agreed in her head. It was too late to charge dead Martin, and any case would not have stood up in court, of that she was sure. If they wanted to prosecute Tom now, well, that would not make her cry.

'Let's move on to TwoBoots. You've already told us that you were friendly with him. Did he have any special friends?'

'No. Everybody was friends with him. I told you he was personable and good at sport. Not bad at classwork either.'

'What about Eddie Murrray?'

Mary thought it a bit remarkable that Eddie's name came up again. She stored it in her memory bank to discuss further with Finn. 'Yeah, no. They weren't special friends. TwoBoots was too popular for any friend to stand out.'

'When did you know TwoBoots had moved away?'

'Straight off. We weren't at all surprised that he got a job in Merimbula and was good at it.'

'Did you see him often after that?'

'Yes, he visited his folks once a month. Never missed.'

'Notice anything unusual about it?'

'Yes. It was always early in the month. Never at the end.'

'Nothing else?'

'No.'

Mary justified that reply as only a mishandling of the truth, not a lie. She wanted the accurate facts extracted from her, not volunteered. She wanted to know how much Paxton knew.

'Did TwoBoots have anything to do with Martin?'

'Well, yes. He talked to Martin every time. He never came up to the house. You can guess why.'

'Did he help with the horses, or was it purely social?'

'Social, I would say.'

'Was Tom Dooley ever there at the same time?'

'Not as a rule. It might have happened sometimes.'

'You've told us you spent a lot of time at the kitchen sink, and not just for the washing up. Was TwoBoots there when the horse trucks were there?'

Jees, thought Mary. He knows. I'd better tread carefully.

'Come to think of it, he was often there when the transporter was.'

'Always?'

'Well, I can't say always. But certainly often. You see, I didn't keep notes. I didn't see any reason to.'

'Let's imagine for a minute that it was always, without fail. What then?'

'Sweet Jesus!' exclaimed Mary, looking at Finnbar, 'That'd mean he was implicated in something. But what? The big horse scam happened only twice in three years. That's hardly enough reason for TwoBoots to be there each month.' She thought that she really should stop cussing like Finn.

'What conclusion do you draw from what I have just told you?'

'He was helping Martin sell dodgy horses! Well I never! Tom Dooley, yes. But TwoBoots – never.'

'Let's move on. Did it ever occur to you that Martin ingested strychnine in the sheds?'

'I was surprised when the postmortem showed Martin died from that poison. Police would jump to the obvious conclusion – murder, by me. Not me, I repeat. Not me. You must have found something down in the sheds.'

Paxton ignored the question. 'Were the sheds locked?'

'Only the tack room full of horse gear. It was also the tool shed. In the other shed, there was only feed in the drums with lids on to keep mice and rats off. Rodents were still all over the place because horses are messy eaters as they toss their heads and snort away the dust up their noses. You wet the feed in their buckets to lay the dust but it's never one hundred per cent. Delivered feed went straight into drums. Bags didn't stop rodents.'

'What would stop them?'

'Rat poison.'

'In other words, strychnine.'

'So you told me the other day. And I bet forensics showed no rat poison in the house. But I bet they found plenty in the sheds.'

'I accept that you didn't spread rat poison down there. Who do you reckon might've?'

'No comment, Mary. You shouldn't speculate.'

'No comment.'

'Where did TwoBoots stand when the transporters were there?'

'As far as I can remember he didn't stand for long. I saw him walking around.'

'How did TwoBoots get to your place? In his own vehicle?'

'I can't vouch for that.'

'Were there ever other men there at the same time?'

'Yes, of course. Sale day was Martin's busy day.'

'So he could have come there in a vehicle other than his own?'

'For sure. I couldn't read number plates from that distance. And please don't ask me for the vehicle brands. I'm a mere female and that doesn't come in a woman's job description. I couldn't even say for sure what brand of ute I drove to the supermarket. Martin filled it up. He didn't trust me not to put petrol into that diesel. As if.'

'Anything else come to mind?'

'No. Why?'

'Did no other man stand out there?'

'No. In what way?'

'Did you ever notice a big man?'

Mary wondered briefly how to answer that question without it leading to protracted questioning. She had already warned Finn that on no account was she going to go there. She would but only when she was good and ready. 'Martin was a big man. Even bigger than Finn here.'

Paxton didn't notice her evasiveness but wasn't sure where to go next. He had hoped to steer her towards opening up about the big man, without revealing first what he knew. He and Wilson were most keen to bring into play the suspicious big footprints. He pondered which of the two should start to show their hand. He thought it better if Wilson led. That way if it failed to elicit anything useful, it would not reflect badly on him.

'Nothing further from me for the moment. I'll hand over now to DI Wilson, leader of the investigation.'

Wilson began, 'Would it surprise you that we found sets of very big footprints down there? Size fourteens.'

'Yes, it would. Finn here is a big man, but I know he was not walking around there.' Finn said that he wore only size thirteens.

'Let's not talk for practice. We are not talking about your legal advisor's feet. We are talking about someone that hopefully you can shed light on. And could shed light on a murder.'

'Sorry,' said Mary, with just the right degree of contriteness, and downcast expression.

'Is there another very big man, apart from Finn here, and of course your late husband, that it could be?'

'No. There were no giants in high school. That is not to say some boys might not have grown bigger later.'

That mode of expression was not totally clear to Wilson. 'Let me be clear, you mean some boys could have kept growing after high school?'

'For sure that was possible. I can't confirm it though, because after I married I was virtually out of circulation. It would be sheer luck if I ran into someone I knew in the half hour or so that it took me to do the food shopping.'

Wilson knew that he had reached a dead end with this line of attack. It was time to reveal his hand. Mary had hoped this all along. Somehow it felt as though the chess game were starting afresh, with her playing white pieces for a change.

'Paxton here has unearthed interesting things by careful investigation.'

Mary thought, *More likely forensics, but no matter. Let's just hope Wilson speaks up.*

'A big man has been standing around while horses were being loaded. Any thoughts why?'

'No.'

'At the same time, TwoBoots was standing around. Any thoughts why?'

Who the hell has been talking? wondered Mary. That group of men up to nothing good would hardly be dobbing on each other. Martin is dead, so it leaves only TwoBoots and the big man. And that really leaves only the big man, and they don't know who he is. No, there has to be some other way. Ahaa! Albert King, the neighbour. That Koori had eyesight beyond belief.

'You've got me bluffed. TwoBoots tell you?'

Wilson ignored the question. Mary knew he would. 'We just have to confirm what we have as evidence. Sure you can't confirm that TwoBoots and the big man talked?'

'I can't confirm it, but clearly they would have talked if they were both here at the same time.'

Wilson knew he had to play the next card from up his sleeve. 'Now, here's something we are revealing outside police circles for the first time.'

Mary rubbed her hands together in anticipation, metaphorically of course. Her face betrayed nothing of her eager anticipation.

'Was it raining when you left in such a hurry?'

'Struth. Let me think. I was travelling light, nothing from here I valued anyway. Come to think of it, I was annoyed at having to use a Drizabone.'

'What's that?'

'A bushman's raincoat, split down the back so you can ride a horse in the rain.'

'So it was raining. I thought so. We have checked all the rainfall records. It was a bit after that we got the postmortem results. Strychnine. Paxton came straight here and put crime scene tape up. Now, here is the interesting part, TwoBoots' footprints were already baked into the mud and all over the place. Why would he be here so soon after Martin's death, snooping around?'

Mary was genuinely flabbergasted, and said so. 'I'd love to help, but I really have no idea. It seems to me that once we know the answer to that particular riddle, we are well on the way to solving both scam and dodgy horse deals. Maybe even murder, although I don't see him as murderer.'

'Mary, it's up to the police to solve the crimes. We'll be in touch if we need you any further. We would like to thank you for your cooperation and help so far.' They took their leave of the police with handshakes all around. The duo went straight up the hill behind the Thredbo Street station to home before starting to talk to each other. Mary pulled out a frozen dinner to thaw, before they both went through the shower ritual.

She had a plentiful supply of nibbles from the deli, to eat with drinks. 'This is as good as lunch, and cheaper for you, Finn,' came out with a smile.

Mary had on a third outfit, this time a jumpsuit like Dianna Rigg in The Avengers. Finn came out looking nothing like Patrick McNee in his bowler hat and black suit. Finn came out in his version of cool – sloppy joe and jeans. Mary thought he looked fetching, and said so. Better than lawyer pinstripe worn even at home, for heaven's sake.

They seemed to lose momentum without the motivation afforded by an interview next day. They found it hard to stick to subject. Once their productivity reached zero, they gave up. The solution wasn't hard to find. Finn would go back to Moola Moola via Sydney. Mary also went to Sydney on the same flight out of the Cooma airport. A call to judge's chambers found a willing Carmel. She would join Finn and Jennifer – or should that be Mary? – for a long talk in a restaurant that Carmel was to arrange.

Carmel was dying to meet up with her old school friend Jen. She had also been missing Finn.

The Next Move

Getting Carmel and Mary together at the same table was like having Deep Blue on your side. That IBM computer was the first to beat a grand master at chess. At that gathering, Finn provided the gravitas of a slightly more senior lawyer than Carmel. In reality, all three felt like they were one and the same generation.

Neither Carmel nor Mary had ever deferred to Finn on account of age. It's doubtful they ever deferred to anyone. Each brought something different to the table. All three at the same table? Now that's like having the big array telescope that helped take the first photograph of the big black hole at the centre of our Milky Way Galaxy. Sagittarius A*.

Carmel had sequestered the trio in her favourite restaurant. No legal folk gathered here. No likelihood of bewigged interruption. No horsehair, joked Mary. Carmel would not need to explain to anyone the earnest tête-à-tête that Friday afternoon and late into the dark.

'We'll go Dutch,' said Mary. For once, only Finn got the joke.

It was quite touching, Mary and Carmel in a hug for the first time in over ten years. Each wiped away a backhand tear with the knuckle of the curled up right digit. Finn wondered what women did with left-handed tears. And then for the first time Carmel hugged Finn. It made him wonder, but he liked the sensation. Irish were not given to hugging.

Better still, Mary followed suit. Finn wondered why, but

thought, *I'll take it when I can get it.* Come to think, they were his first hugs since he arrived in Australia as a callow youth. Mary's scent lingered. Finn inhaled the aftertaste. He tried to exhale smaller than inhale for quite a while.

Niceties over and teardrops dried, they started their real business. Finn told the story from his perspective. Mary confirmed exactly how she had reached the stage of getting Mahoney & Geeves to finish her legal name change. Carmel chimed in with her role in the affair, if that was the right word. It didn't take long for that assemblage of brain power to get the full jigsaw. Carmel broke that peace soon enough.

'Jen, I mean, Mary, there's still a piece missing.'

Finn was a bit surprised because he couldn't see what was missing. Mary had detailed grandma's legacy of De Beers best, the false scent the fox had laid to escape the hounds, the bank drafts, the cook's tour of the Australian coast, the house purchase in West Perth, the establishment of the coffee machine business. That had prompted his, 'Some coffee shop you run, Mary!'

He applauded how she had run ragged the coppers' sleuthing. How they made it most of the way, but not all the way. How he stood in awe of her barrister-skill in manoeuvring the police to reveal their hand. This gave them tactical advantage for the next step. And most of all, how skilful Mary had been in revealing not very much to the police at her interrogation. Just enough for them to think her honest, which she had been. Her fibs were acts of omission, not commission. You can't be convicted for that.

Mary, 'Why didn't you praise me like this before?' Broad flash of flapper red, pearly whites, deep dimple.

Finn, 'I didn't want you to fall in love!' His ha ha made that comment okay. Joke taken. But Carmel jealoused just a tad.

'Finally, we have arrived at this meeting of minds, knowing what the next steps of the law might be. They don't know what this little coven of thirteen minus ten is up to.' He didn't have to explain the origin of bad luck associated with the number thirteen.

Carmel knew that he was joking about the number of witches of Salem, but nevertheless said, 'I don't appreciate being likened a witch. Nor would Mary of Eva. We will neither hang nor drown.' That made the trio laugh a bit.

Finn continued, 'If you ask me, having been tinking as I speak, there is still a bit of a mystery about why the police hadn't found you before you "handed yourself in" so to speak. I will never forget the look on Sergeant Paxton's face when you said, "I am Mrs Jennifer O'Hanlon to you. To Mr Mahoney, I am Mary Flamboya!" Tell you the truth, I wish I could have seen my own face at that moment. I still don't know why you told them that when you didn't have to. I was not going to reveal that. You must have known.'

Carmel, 'I know why. And that leads me to my question about something missing in your narrative.'

Mary simply replied, 'Carmel, I know you would figure it out. We women function best on intuition. Mere males are always in our dust.'

Bait bait bait, thought Finn, but refrained from saying it out loud. He was not going to bite. *She can go fish elsewhere.*

Carmel then laid out her thinking with surgical precision. Or should that be, 'like a barrister'? 'You disappeared we didn't know exactly how. Now we know ninety nine percent. With what you have told us, I could find the missing piece in the jigsaw easily enough. I would search ships' registers for the date you left. It would be a narrow search because I would only have to visit Newcastle. With your date, I don't have to even know the name of the ship. You have conveniently not told us that. There would only be a few sailings that day out of Newcastle.'

'Getting hot,' said Mary.

Finn's eyes narrowed. He was starting to get this. Mary said, 'The penny's starting to drop with Finnbar. Just look at his eyes.'

'Bingo! When I found the ship that had signed on a new cook.'

'Bingo,' said Mary. 'I signed on as Mary Chiaprisi on the good ship *Mary Ganter*. And that is the name Perth knows me by. Mary Chiaprisi, that is. She is the director of Forza Coffee. Finn is familiar with our stylised coffee bean logo I believe.'

From pursed lips came the first two lines of 'Danny Boy'. 'Yeah, no. The shower cap in your bathroom.'

Carmel looked like a jealous cat. 'You mean you two lived together under the same roof in Jindabyne!'

'Don't worry, Carmel. Relax. We were under a roof of convenience, that's all. We needed to conference each night and prepare for next day's fireworks. I made sure that Finn here couldn't bill me for accommodation. He doesn't understand economics so it was easy to bamboozle him.'

'I told him he could ask for rent, but he would have to claim it as a business expense, and I would have to declare the payment as income and pay tax on it. The taxman would be better off, the GNP would grow by double the same amount, but national welfare would not alter. We mutually agreed to leave the GNP as we found it.'

Carmel, 'That's not lawyer logic, but I like it.' She especially liked the outcome of that little explanation. 'Now I believe we know everything. We don't have to tell the police that Chiaprisi is their man, sorry, woman. They will find out when we are good and ready.'

Where to next was a rhetorical question that hung in the air. The meal arrived and gave them respite to think as they savoured. They asked for a delay between courses. The business talk resumed at this interval.

Carmel broke the ice. 'The police are laying down false scents. We need to eliminate them one by one. When we have only one name, then we go for the jugular. But where do we start? We can't start with the guilty one, because that we will have to deduce, not assume. First render, then solve.'

Mary, 'I'm not expected in Perth for another three weeks, if I choose. I vote that Finn and I go to Mudgee, where we will find Tom Dooley. He won't've worn out his welcome yet. Quite the contrary, Finn and I think. For sure Tom's not guilty of more than petty shit, pardon the French. We can eliminate him once and for all. In the process, we will learn a bit on how to tackle TwoBoots.'

'Who's TwoBoots?' interjected Carmel.

'Sorry. Freddy Ford. He was our classmate at high school, don't you remember?

'Yeah yeah yeah. I'd forgotten in all this excitement.'

Mary said, 'Now, here's how I think Tom Dooley can give us some leads. We know from what the police told us, albeit with a bit of persuasion from me, that Tom was at Martin's quite often but not to a pattern. Freddy Ford was there monthly on Cooma sales day, the second Thursday each month. So it was normal that he came across TwoBoots, who was also there every sale day. And some really big guy. The police kindly told us his size fourteen boots were there too, like clockwork, same days. On the balance of probabilities, Tom would have overhead some of the chat between the big man and TwoBoots.'

'Finn and I can jolly some of that scuttlebutt out of Tom when we get to Mudgee.'

'I agree,' said Carmel as Finn nodded. 'Who is the big man?'

'Carmel, I have a theory, but I'm not ready to share just yet in case I'm way off. I hope that Tom might be able to help.'

Finn jumped in with his two bob's worth. 'Tom was on Martin's payroll, but we don't know what for. It's hardly likely for a real job. Tom hasn't done a proper day's work in his life. We can't see him pulling skeleton weeds or spraying Paterson's curse.

'If Mary and I play it smart, I reckon we can extract the reason for Martin paying Tom. And while we're at it, uncover the big man.' He added, 'Those both tings are so important.'

'*Things*,' teased Mary, '*Things* … Finn.'

'Two good points. Now I don't like to speculate. So why don't we meet again in a couple of days when it suits you? We'll give your love to Mudgee.'

Quaff a Mudgee Red

Australia is blessed with wonderful wine regions – Margaret River, Swan Valley, Barossa Valley, Adelaide Hills, McLaren Vale, Yarra Valley, Mornington Peninsula, Hunter Valley. The list goes on. Mudgee is right up there. Mudgee shiraz is on the lips of every aficionado. Award winning drops and epicurean fare, that's what awaited Finn and Mary. Whiskey could wait.

Mary had never visited. Too young at school. Too shackled by Martin after. This was going to be a treat. Let's hope Tom Dooley wouldn't spoil the taste.

They were booked into Bushman's Cottage, a restored colonial relic near Clayhill Creek that ran through the estate. It would serve them well as they jollied and cajoled Tom to help solve their dilemma. Three nights and two full days, Friday and Saturday, should do the trick. As with all liquor sellers, cellar doors opened at 10:00 a.m.

Imagine their feigned surprise when they greeted Tom at front of house of Pieter van der Harmen Winery and Estate. There was no feign in Tom's surprise. He was actually quite pleased to see them. Here was his chance to show them a changed man.

Since it was quiet as always at opening, Tom cleared with his boss to give this up-market couple the full treatment. It started with a tour of the vineyard and finished in the tasting room. It soon became clear that Tom had finally found his niche. He could gift his gab freely. It was the main part of his job description.

The more he charmed the client, the more impressed was management. This was not *My Fair Lady* stuff, oozing charm from every pore, oiling his way around the floor. Tom was the real McCoy, in a manner of speaking; nature's own.

In between his mellifluous delivery of charming marketing, he convinced management that this was his future. He would put his nose to the grindstone. He didn't need lessons in elocution. He was going to study wine making. He was not going to do anything to spoil his future.

Mary and Finn genuinely wished him well. He was grateful. That duo had actually gone guarantor for this new job. Finn was old mates with Pieter and had pushed him into a really big and risky favour. Finn had once taken him pig hunting in Moola, because he knew how Pieter had loved to hunt in the Ardennes in Belgium.

Finn had said at day's end, 'I'm so happy I didn't have to put down that wild boar. I just couldn't look that creature in the eye.'

Pieter, 'But we didn't see a single pig that day!'

Finn, 'That's what I was so happy about!' How they had laughed.

Mary and Finn together had provided Tom Dooley with a signed referee's report. They had recommended Tom in clear terms. Mahoney & Geeves of Moola Moola and Forza Coffee of Subiaco Perth would be answerable for him. With this comfort, the winery included a little cottage for Tom to live in as part of his employment deal.

For once, a mere male had displayed better intuition than the fair sex. He could divine Tom's future where Mary could not. How many calories in a bowl of hope? It had taken Finn at his persuasive best to convince Mary. Her, on Toe Rag's side! Ruddy youth and arrant scoundrel! Ask that scum! Ask that wastrel! Fitting time for his departure, not arrival.

Finn had sealed it with, blessed are the meek, a Hail Mary or two, and the sign of the cross. Mary had graciously smiled to Finn, 'All you need is a Cardinal's biretta and three scarlet bangs of your staff on the floor.'

Mary had, after all, been raised religious. Prayed white dove render me three precious angels, three, and black raven, devil, none. After three years of devil Martin, of further prayers, none.

'Quoth the Raven "Nevermore"'

Edgar Allan Poe

When they got back to the tasting room, and making sure that management could see, Mary gave Tom a polite hug. She flashed a smile also, dimple side to the boss, and said quietly, 'We'll bring dinner, and you can show us your digs. We are staying at the Bushman's Cottage. Six o'clock.' She didn't wait for a reply. He had no chance to refuse. Tom was like putty in her hands.

They went to the Italian deli in town. That deli would put any city nosherie to shame. The produce around Mudgee was unbelievable. Almost as good as Margaret River, opined Mary. Sandgropers should stick together. They assembled a dinner fit for a king and had it fancy packed. Just to look good at Tom's cabin. Finn refrained from making a joke about that. Mary, reading his mind, said, 'I won't have any racism here, thank you.'

They bought a case of Pieter's finest at his town outlet, as much as they might drink tonight, and if anything was left, Carmel could take it to Sydney.

Six o'clock on the knocker, they knocked on Tom's front door. Or rather, they struck on the horseshoe hung out front, with the big part of a horse's bit. Mary approved. She only wished she had a horse to go with it. It was a bit of a squeeze in that tight space. Tom had arranged the only two chairs he had, one for Mary, one for Finn. For himself, he had a hay bale with a cloth over to blunt the prickles.

On the little kitchen table, Mary called it intimate, he had three plates and ironmongery to suit, three flutes to boot. How was Tom to know they were bringing red? He could easily have borrowed large wine bowls for the red occasion.

Up until now, Tom rationalised that he had struck a streak of bad luck. Truth is, if Tom hadn't made his own bad luck, he wouldn't've had any luck at all. Tom had entirely missed the in between. His card had been marked. This mine host version of Tom was pretty good by his crab apple standards. Gone was his culture of aimlessness. Manifest destiny took its place.

Mary served the food onto the plates, from the small bench left over after two antique gas rings had taken their permanent station on that horizontal space. Two wine bottles had to be satisfied with the side table by the single seater couch. She got Finn to open the two for breathing purposes. 'Mudgee shiraz tastes best that way,' Tom Dooley glad-handed the guests.

Mary had forewarned Finn. Tom was to be the major quaffer that evening. Without his knowing it. The guests were to take perfunctory sips. Reloading was Finn's job, because the haybale was somewhat trapped behind the table. And Tom with it. Now, who would have arranged that?

Finn did the first pour, after the red had breathed its quota. Two flutes had a meniscus quite lower than the third. It was not obvious, with the speed that the guests had wrapped their delicate forefingers just at the Plimsoll line, raised their glasses, clinked Tom's, and got down to the real business of the evening.

Mary opened, 'Tom, you know and you know that we know that you have a chequered past. Looks like you've taken this opportunity with both hands.'

Tom, 'I know. I really don't know how I landed this job. I never imagined that full time work could be this good. I wake up with the magpies and then it's all go from there. And the boss, Mr van der Harmen, has got me started on courses for winemaking. It's a start, but I understand that I have to get all sorts of certificates before I can start at wine school proper.'

Finn stepped in all business like, 'Tom, I won't beat about the bush. It's stick your neck out time. You're a clever young man, and it's great to see the start you've made. It's a bit later than usual, but the way you are throwing yourself into it, there's no doubt in my mind that you will make it. You were who you were and now you're not. Now you can seek out good trouble.

'Now, you would know why I have been pulled into the police investigation of Martin's murder. Mary here is Jennifer Spring, your classmate from years ago. As Martin's wife, she is right in the firing line. Anything you know would be a great help in my preparing her defence. I doubt it's going to get that far. With your help, Mary should not long remain a suspect.'

Raised glasses, one quaff and two sips. The Plimsoll lines matched. Easy to see since the glasses were now quite close to each other. Finn now made a show of reloading them, Tom's to a finger's width from the top, the other two another two fingers below. This time the glasses settled quite a way apart. A couple more 'Here's to us's' and the truth serum would have worked its magic. And they ate till they were sated, drank the wine in full contentment.

'The police have put Mary through the wringer. She's come through in my estimate with flying colours. We're a bit stuck at the bit where Mary has told the police what she has seen from too many years stuck at the kitchen sink. It has that big window behind that looks down to the stables, sheds and loading yards.

'The biggest unknown is, just why was Freddy Ford there on each and every Cooma stock sales day? You weren't there so regularly, but Mary did see you talking to TwoBoots quite often.'

'I was basically told by TwoBoots when to come. At first it seemed just to have a catch up. It took a while for the penny to drop. I was being set up for something. Not quite sure what, so

I started to pump Freddy. You know I can talk when needs be.'

Mary thought, *Needs be, is all the time.* She refrained from the obvious. He had dealt with the powers that be by yessing them to death. Pissing them off in the process. Getting marching orders in return.

'For a while I was flattered that it was to set up an alibi for me. You know that I think of myself first sometimes.'

Always, thought Mary but to herself only. *This is going really well.*

'I thought that I was being set up to commit something somewhere for TwoBoots, but if it was ever found out, it could be proved that I was here.'

'Now at length we're coming somewhere. Did you tell the detectives this?' interrupted Finn.

'Yes. But I have been thinking since that this was not correct. Mind, I didn't lie to them. I just had not worked it out.'

'Are you prepared to tell us now what you know?' Mary dimpled. She and Finn knew that Mudgee's truth serum made that a foregone conclusion. They knew that Tom was street smart, moreso than clever.

Tom had the smarts to say, 'Promise you will never reveal your source?'

They had no trouble promising. And what's more, they promised to themselves that they never would. But they triumphed inside. The next interview with the detectives would be in Moola Moola, bless their cotton pickin' socks. It was time to put some sleep in the bank.

Boot Pressure

Freddy Ford did as he was summoned, and fronted Detective Inspector Wilson and Sergeant Paxton at the Thredbo Street cop shop. He was understandably nervous. What would they manage to extract from him? He was unrepresented but had briefed a solicitor in Merimbula. If necessary, Freddy was to request a delay in proceedings until he had the solicitor beside him.

Wilson made no attempt to make Freddy comfortable. Quite the contrary. He put the full array of his bully tactics into play, leaning aggressively forward. 'Why were you at Martin O'Hanlon's place?'

'Because Tom Dooley invited me.'

'Every time?'

'Yes.'

'Are you sure?'

Freddy grew a little nervous. 'Yes, most times.'

He thought that a little insurance was in order. The next question had him searching for a much bigger insurance policy. 'How often was Tom Dooley there?'

'Most times, I guess.'

'What does most times mean? More than fifty per cent or less than fifty?'

'I don't know.'

'Well let me tell you, it was a lot less than fifty per cent. Anything you would like to re-state?'

'Yes. Now that I think of it, Tom wasn't there all that often.'

'What's your explanation for your change of heart?'

'I guess I mis-spoke.'

'Fine. Now, I can tell you what we have found out. You were there once a month every month, early each month on the second Thursday. Tom Dooley only intermittently. What happens each second Thursday of the month?'

'It's busy day at Martin O'Hanlon's.'

'Now, I advise you not to get smart with me. Why was it busy day at Martin's?'

'Stock sales day at Cooma.'

'We could have saved time if you just came straight out and said so. You may have, but I don't have, time to waste. Same goes for Sergeant Paxton here. Now, can we have straight answers to straight questions? And I'm not saying please.'

Freddy Ford grew decidedly nervous. This was not going well. He recalled his solicitor's advice about giving short direct answers. Not to qualify anything. Not to give room for doubt. And it would be best if I were there to protect your interests. From what you have told me – and I feel as if you are holding back – you have something to hide. And you give out that feeling. Imagine what the detectives will make of you. They are used to interrogations of many people on the same subject. When they piece it all together, they also know a lie when they see one. You are lucky so far that you are just a person of interest. If you were a suspect, they would charge you with whatever, and the evidence from the questioning would be presented in court. If you lie under oath there, you could be charged with perjury and perverting the course of justice. Even if you were innocent of the charge, you could do time in gaol. Perjury is regarded as a serious crime.

Unfortunately, Freddy had ignored this mini lecture. How he regretted it now.

'I want an adjournment until tomorrow. I'd like to have a solicitor please.'

'I'll call him in now.'

Freddy was about to protest. Before the words came out of his mouth, in walked Stan Smith of Smith & Smith, Merimbula.

'I'll explain later. Now, what have we here?' Surely Freddy did not need an explanation. But then again, none so blind as he who will not see.

Smith was very professional, and Wilson muted his tone quite a bit. There would be no more intimidation from here on. In fact, Wilson asked Freddy if he wanted something to drink. Smith answered for him, 'Two white coffees please. And I hope they are good ones.'

Wilson groaned to himself. *Now where have I heard that before?*

The memory of Mary Flamboya flooded back, a Pavlovian response to any mention of the quality of the coffee. It was nothing to do with the instant crap the police station had to contend with. Their budget did not stretch to a mini Faema, even at the trade price Mary had offered. And her knowing eyes, even in their downcast mode, continued to haunt him. It had everything to do with the ease with which she had reversed the tables. He felt as if he were the one being questioned.

He knew he shouldn't be feeling like that because there was only one Mary Flamboya. He quickly corrected himself. Make that three, with Eva Britten and Carmel Blount. Luckily, one in one place, one in another, a third in Sydney. And that Irishman didn't make things any easier either. Little did he know that he was to meet that quartet again all too soon.

'Now, Mr Ford, you were at the O'Hanlon's each second Thursday of the month. Correct?'

'Yes.'

'Was there anyone else that was there each time?'

'Yes.'

'Names please.'

Tom rattled off Martin and Bumfluff and the names of the truck drivers, but they were there only if contracted by the seller. Otherwise Martin drove himself, and occasionally Bumfluff.

'We know that size fourteen boots was also there. Correct?'

'Yes.'

Wilson showed his exasperation. 'What is his name?'

'I don't know.'

'Is it Eddie Murray?'

'Hell no. I haven't seen Eddie since the whole family moved to somewhere in the Southern Highlands, I think.'

Wilson's shoulders sank visibly. He had been sure that the big man would emerge with a name attached when they had finished with Ford. He just had to get on with it. 'What was the big man doing there?'

'He would always pump me for information. Who did what to whom and who was not paying. That sort of stuff. At first it didn't make much sense to me. Bit by bit I got the feeling that he was establishing an alibi for himself. Something that would happen somewhere else on a second Thursday.'

'Any idea what that might be?'

A 'no comment' came from Smith. 'You cannot be expected to speculate.'

'No comment.' Freddy was beginning to see how this all worked.

It was Sergeant Paxton's turn. 'Was the big man there when the six stolen horses went to the saleyards?'

'Yes. Like I said, he was always there.'

'Was anything said when Martin went to gaol over that?'

'Hell yes. We all wondered how the police managed to pin that onto Martin. As far as we could see, all the paperwork was in order. We couldn't see how Martin could have been a forger. The big man never talked about it. Made me suspicious he had something to do with it.'

Paxton wanted to avoid too much talk of this embarrassing episode of police incompetence.

'Did you have anything to do with it?'

Smith, 'You don't have to incriminate yourself.'

'No comment.'

'Were you ever at the O'Hanlon place other than second Thursdays?'

This caught Freddy by total surprise. The Nakamichi reeled on, recording every nuance, even the fast breathing of Freddy that kept pace with his now elevated heartrate. How on earth could they know? He took out a small insurance policy with his reply, 'I may have been.'

'Let me answer that for you. You were there as soon as Jennifer O'Hanlon had disappeared for good. Correct?'

'Yes.' Smith had a look on his face that expressed surprise. His client had said nothing about this during their briefings. He knew what was coming next. Freddy knew they had him. But who had talked? He had gone there on his own. He had told no one.

Freddy stuttered a bit in his reply. 'I was looking for something that I had left behind.'

'Where did you look? At the house? At the stables? In the yards? In the tack shed?'

'Around the yards.'

'Are you sure?'

Freddy's voice betrayed his 'not so sure'.

'Your footprints were everywhere, around the house, the yards, the tack room, the round yard, the dressage arena. What was so important for you to search so thoroughly?'

'Sir, can I have a bit of time out with Mr Smith?'

'Of course. We'll break for lunch. Back here at 1:00 p.m. sharp.'

Over fish and chips down by the lake with begging squarking fighting seagulls, Freddy told Smith how each sales day Thursday of the month he kept a notebook where he recorded things that seemed suspicious to him. It had names and everything. It was the thing that most had to be kept secret. If it fell into the wrong hands, it would be a great risk to him. Who knows what 'they' would do?

Back at afternoon interview, Smith opened with, 'I have advised my client that he can reveal the reason why he was there.'

Freddy addressed himself to Paxton, who obviously was the one who had discovered the footprints. He described in detail everything that was in that notebook. He was very afraid that if it fell into the wrong hands, who knows what could happen to him?

'Thank you, Freddy. DI Wilson and I have no further questions. You may go. We will do a search ourselves for your missing notebook. It is very important evidence for us, if we can find it. If it ever existed.'

The Big Man Part Two

When Finn and Mary lunched at the Royal George Hotel on high plains payday, they got more than just a lunch and a new experience. Mary had projected her unease at seeing the big man. The one with the flaming red Ned Kelly beard down to his belly button. Probably the Ned's heritage, too, going by the beard colour. Finn's countryman from way back.

She hoped that he had not noticed her flicker of recognition. He had noticed as they ever so briefly locked eyes. But Mary had passed him by before his flicker of recognition might register back at her. He was not afraid of any consequences, like Mary was. The menace was all his, starting with his gigantic stature and unkempt beard. He liked it that way. With his beard in position, nobody could see what he was thinking.

The fear was all hers.

With the protection that went with his menace, plus iron hard fitness begat of hard work, the big man put it all aside until his brain cells returned to normal after the payday bash. Then he set to thinking. It was Martin's wife, he felt sure. She looked completely different, dressed completely different, looked like city folk do, walked like a softie, but sure as hell, it was her!

He remembered that when Martin went off to gaol Jennifer had simply disappeared. And now detectives were in town interviewing all 'persons of interest'. And he didn't want to join their ranks. Not for love nor money. He felt innocent of involvement in Martin's poisoning, but that wouldn't stop the cops from trying to pin something on him. He knew how hard it was to prove something that didn't happen.

That must be why Jennifer was in town. He really would like to talk to her. He would like to do that before the inevitable happened, before he was called in for questioning. His remote workplace could protect him only so far, because on paydays he had to go to town.

He thought that a pre-emptive strike was the only way to protect himself. He planned his next move thoroughly. He talked around the pub about the big man who was Jennifer's lawyer. Well, not as big as himself but big enough. He drank more water than beer, if indeed he drank booze at all. Some of his mates there asked if he was feeling unwell. It wasn't hard to pin a name on the suave one's back. Town gossip had seen to that.

Next day the big man phoned Mahoney & Geeves and stated his business with the receptionist. He really needed to speak urgently with Mr Mahoney. She readily gave a telephone number where he might be contacted. She did not know when Mr Mahoney might be back in the office. He would be sure to help your urgent case over the phone. It will have to be afterhours when you call. During the day he will be otherwise engaged.

At six o'clock that night, the phone rang in the Bushman's Cottage. 'Finnbar Mahoney speaking.'

The soft-spoken voice on the phone belied his stature. It was the sort of voice that a puppy would run to and kittens would cuddle. 'You don't know me except by description. You would have seen me with my red beard at the Royal George a payday ago. I also saw your offsider, the beautiful one. I believe she may have recognised me.'

The big man wondered why he was being serenaded by whistled Irish airs that his grandmother had taught him. He whistled back a bar of another of grandma's favourites.

Finnbar stopped his whistling. 'How may I help you?'

'I need to see you with the greatest urgency. My information has to do with Martin O'Hanlon's death. I can be in Mudgee tomorrow, Saturday morning. Would it be convenient to meet you at ten?'

Sweet mother of Jesus and an endless supply of Hail Marys. 'Of course. Here are the directions to the Bushman's Cottage, at the Pieter van der Harmen Winery and Estate.' Mary nearly fell over backwards at Finn's news. The mountain was coming to Mohammet! The big man himself was coming to them!

'Who could protect us if he ran amok,' was Mary's concern. Then she set about briefing Finn on her latest discovery. The notebook.

'What kept you so long?' was his rather sarcastic comment.

'Finn, you aren't married, so you don't know about handbags. Nor do you have kids, so little boys' pockets likewise, with their sticks and stones and snail shells. I'd like to be there the day you find out. Or do you still remember?'

She told him of how she did one last reconnoitre of the farm before she left. The horses had been sold but all the same she did one last circuit. She found a notebook at the back of the round yard and put it in her pocket. It started to rain. She forgot all about it with the business of running away. It went into her shoulder bag and was lost in the mess of bits and bobs therein.

Scrabbling around last night in her bedroom, just after the phone call, what was there amongst the scrabbled paraphernalia but the notebook! She sat up late in bed going through it. Some of it was easy enough, but some was in a code of sorts. And now one of the coded ones was coming to them at ten tomorrow. The big man!

Finn looked through the notebook, and soon deciphered the author. TwoBoots! What the! Finn said we don't tell the big man about the existence of this notebook. And we can't tell Freddy Ford, aka TwoBoots. It's quite clear that each suspects the other of skullduggery.

Neither Mary nor Finn could wait for tomorrow. It's all very well strumming away like the Travelling Wilburys. You've got to pin a tail on the donkey.

Revelation

At around 10:00 a.m., a dusty 4X4 ute with a kelpie in the back pulled up in a cloud of dust. It was a bit hard to distinguish the dust from the ute, the ute from the dust. When it had settled, a figure unfolded – that is the only word – from within. It unfolded and unfolded until it was about two metres and a bit tall. Six foot seven in old money.

Two axe handles across or so it seemed, and the hips seemed too slim to hold those shoulders up. He was so big that if he reversed, he would have to beep like a truck. He banged a dusty rabbit felt fur hat on his head, battered from under countless horse hooves, probably an Akubra back in the day. Or should that be, in better days.

The tangle of flame red covered his features under that hat and did its best to also cover his torso. It was lucky he could still get at his belt, with its horseshoe buckle made of solid brass. It incorporated a bottle opener to save opening the second drawer down in the kitchen, when a thirst erupted without warning.

Surprisingly, his legs were not much bowed. Those tree trunk thighs were too strong for even a horse to persuade them out of their God-given birth shape. The triple stitched jeans with double arse and double knees did a poor job of containing all that mass of muscle. And then the big man spoke. His voice was soft and gentle as a summer breeze, the tone soothing, no menace.

'I am Clancy O'Mee. Pleased I be meeting you.'

'Finnbar Mahoney. Pleasing it is. This is Mary Flamboya. I believe you may have met already.'

Mary thought. You can never take the Irish out of the boys. She offered her tiny hand, just to see what it felt like. That paw was gentle but could easily crush hers if the wrong occasion arose. 'We have met but we have not been introduced. I was Jennifer O'Hanlon. You would not have seen me at the farm, but I was there, banished to the kitchen by my husband. You would have known the bastard. I certainly could not miss you each Cooma stock sales day.'

'I have that effect on people,' gentled Clancy.

Mary wondered if that rustle in the beard signified a smile. She reckoned that at least a trim around the teeth area would make for cleaner beer drinking. She remembered the foam-encrusted sleeve back in the payday pub.

Clancy said, 'I am afraid, really afraid. I can't get the shark music from *Jaws* out of my head. That is why I am here.'

Mary thought, *Surely that beard can't be hiding a weak chin?* She wasn't game to be saying that out loud though. It might just be chiselled like the granite chin of Chesty Bond of singlet fame. Clancy was wearing a cotton one that once would have been white. Now of indeterminate colour, the singlet was stretched taut and struggling to provide adequate coverage. Tight around the hirsute ginger armpits too.

Instead, she said, 'Let's go inside. We have a good coffee, the best that a mini Faema has to offer. Breakfast too if you like.'

'I could eat a horse and chase the rider.'

'How many eggs?'

'Six please, and lots of bacon. And some water for me dog.'

Mary smiled and dimpled. 'Just as well the chickens are laying well. I'll fetch fresh laid ones from the henhouse.' There was no fear in the air. Quite the opposite.

As Clancy was addressing his hunger, Finn took the opportunity to fill in with all the details that he saw fit to reveal. It was most everything, save the notebook. It was prudent for that to stay in wraps for a while.

'In summary, Clancy, you are more than just a person of interest to the investigating team. It's because nobody knows your name, nor why you were at the O'Hanlon's each sales day. You've done well to contact me first. Together with my little team, we can plan for your interview with the police.

'Another coffee? No? Then we can start. Why were you there at sales days?'

'I had to go to the O'Hanlon's once on behalf of my boss who was selling some yearlings. It went so well that he had some horses on consignment every time after.

'No worries at the start. Then that guy with boots of two different sizes started to chat me up. I knew him but he didn't know me. I got the impression pretty fast that he was trying to use me as an alibi for something shifty going on somewhere else. I never found out what, but that feeling never went away. Never. And then when Martin died – he had been looking crooker and crooker over a fair while – I got really worried. That's why I am so afraid now. Are they going to pin murder on me?'

Finnbar cut in just as Mary was about to speak. By now she was used to him. She was not offended, knowing that with his lawyer hat on he spoke only when he had something to say. 'I can be sure that that will never happen. TwoBoots thought that you were trying to set him up, to give you him as an alibi for something you were doing on the side.'

'Well, I never. So we each suspected the other of something untoward, serious as it turned out when Martin died of strychnine poisoning. We're both innocent then?'

'It looks that way, but we still have to tread carefully with the police. If neither of you did it, the question remains, whodunnit?

They won't stop until they have a conviction. And their processes are not always pretty.

'The police are interviewing TwoBoots as we speak. I reckon they will be trying to heavy him into a confession. Now you have convinced me that he didn't do it, that you didn't do it, so we need to work on how to proceed when the cops interview you. That is bound to happen soon. I think we should get in first, put them off balance, and have them come on Monday to my office in Moola where we will have home ground advantage.

'Can we drive straight from here tomorrow to Moola? Can you get the time off work? I'll phone the police station in Jindabyne straight away with an offer DI Wilson can't refuse. Paxton should be able to come, no, make that itching, and penny to a pound Merton will be only too happy to have a break from the Sydney office.'

'No worries. I've got plenty of leave up me sleeve. It's quiet time now, so it suits the boss as well. Can I use the phone in this cabin?'

'Go ahead. With your permission, I will have Mary at the same interview. The two of you will be more than a match for the police.'

Finn refrained from saying out loud where the real match would come from. Mary had sat quiet through the morning's proceedings, but now spoke up. Clancy was so glad she was on his side, and said so. Mary merely flashed a dimple. Finn liked that version, the one that signified trust and friendship. Not the one that meant, 'Watch out, I'll get you'.

Mary clarified her position to give comfort to the big man, 'Clancy, you and TwoBoots and I can rest easy because we know that we are innocent. The same goes for Tom Dooley, but I believe the police have already taken him off their list.

'On Monday I can vouch for the times you were at our place. I have already told them how I have done my own detective work.

I have compared all the paperwork for stock transported from my place to Cooma, reconciled it with the banking, the transport chits, everything. It proves that any funny business was done by someone, likely somewhere else, that I can't prove. The police may never prove it either.

'Each time they ask you a question, Finn here will interject on our behalf if they are trying to get us to incriminate ourselves. Believe me, they failed over three days with me. I made the cops look a bit stupid, just ask Finn. I now know everything that the cops know. They revealed it by their line of questioning. The only unknown is what TwoBoots has told them as they apply the thumbscrews. Smith of Smith & Smith Merimbula is quite capable of looking after Freddy Ford's best interests.'

'Jees,' interrupted Clancy, 'Is that what his real name is?"

'Now, all of us were at high school together so know each other very well. Tom has a reputation as a petty repeat offender, but Finn and I know that even he has turned over a new leaf.

'Did you get to talk to Tom?'

'If I could get a word in edgewise. Didn't trust him, that's for sure. I could not work out why he was there. In the end, the only explanation was that he was trying to use TwoBoots and me as an alibi. That didn't make sense to me. Why would you have a trio setting up three-way alibis? You know what they say, "Three's a crowd". So, the more I thought about it, the surer I was that Tom his self was being set up as an alibi by someone else. Not someone like us at sales day.'

Mary noted 'his self' with an inner smile. More evidence you can never take the Irish out of the boy, ha ha.

Finn said, and Mary concurred, that the only other name that they could come up with was Eddie Murray. His whole family had moved to the Southern Highlands or the Illawarra when he was halfway through high school, and no one had seen hide nor hair of him since.

What Clancy said next was a shock to both of them, 'I am Eddie Murray!'

'What!' escaped from Mary and Finn, 'Please explain.'

Before he could, Mary exclaimed, 'When Irish eyes are smiling. I would know those eyes anywhere. So you must have grown a lot after fifteen. Without that beard, I'd have known you anywhere.'

'My parents split soon after we arrived. A bit later Mum married Brendan O'Mee. Now my birth certificate showed me as Clancy Edward Murray. I adopted my mum's name. It was easier not to have to explain at my new school. I liked the sound, so kept my birth first name. So now I'm Clancy O'Mee. It turns out to be the perfect name for the Snowy Mountains.'

'Wow!' That was the first time Mary had ever heard Finn use that expression. Finn preferred by far to express amazement by whistle.

'Mary and I and Eva and Carmel have built up a stock of information on this case. Quite a bit we have not yet told to the police. Now we are in a position of real strength. We know what they don't. It's for us to know and for them to find out.

'Monday is that day. I was going to keep our powder dry on one thing, but it's time to tell you. TwoBoots kept a notebook, which he lost at Mary's. We have that notebook. It proves that Mary and Tom and Clancy here are all innocent. Clancy, you can read it, to give you comfort that Monday will be just fine.'

'I remember Eva, but who's Carmel? Do I know her?'

'Carmel Blount. She and I were best mates at high school. She's a judge's associate in Sydney now. We have to be careful about how we involve her. Conflict of interest and all that. But I'll manoeuvre DI Wison into insisting she be at Moola on Monday morning.'

'I remember her a bit. Always top of class, at least when I was there.'

'And when you weren't, Clancy. She has never been any less. And bet you the price of dinner tonight she will never be anything else.'

Finn, 'Never bet against Mary. Now, could you make that phone call?'

Mary dialled the police station using the latest push button dial. The constable answered, but on hearing that it was Mary Flamboya was eager to put Wilson on. Her fame was all over the police station. Not someone to be messed with.

'DI Wilson, how good it is to talk with you again.' She could almost hear the groan at the other end. 'We have things of interest that will make you look good later.'

What's the catch? When is Mary not out to catch me? He thought those words but never said them. 'Go on.'

'We've pumped Tom Dooley dry. He has been very interesting. Finn and I have made notes and will type out a statement once we get back to Moola.'

'*Back* to Moola? Where are you.?'

'In Mudgee. Tom has a steady job here.'

'I'll believe that when I see it with my own eyes.'

'I thought that too, but I'm a believer, not a doubt in my mind. We also have a notebook that TwoBoots kept interesting stuff in. We, I mean Finn, is treating what it contains as privileged information, between client and lawyer. I don't have to tell you what that means. You could subpoena it, but only for court proceedings. It need not come to that. We can allude to that information in another way.'

Bloody hell. Now she alludes, for chrissake. She was never afraid to pick up the cudgel and start issuing it. Around our features. Not out loud of course.

It didn't have to be out loud. Finn noticed her 'gotcha' dimple.

Clancy was brought down to size also. 'And she reckons Carmel is top of class. I hope I never have to tangle with either.'

Finn said, 'That you will, and to be sure, soon enough. Carmel will be there Monday as well!'

Mary again to Wilson, 'We are prepared to talk about it on Monday, but without revealing confidence between client and lawyer. Have we got a deal?'

God help me, thought Wilson. *So light hearted, so deep and meaningful*. Then out loud, 'I still need persuading.'

'I thought you'd say that. We will also have with us the big man.'

'Well, I never. What's his name?'

'Clancy O'Mee.'

'Hell, I was hoping you'd say Eddie Murray.'

Mary said nothing to that.

'Now, we can only get our side together in the offices of Mahoney & Geeves in Moola Moola. Have we got a deal?'

Wilson knew what the Christmas grip felt like. He meekly said yes.

'Oh, and we want DS Merton and Sergeant Paxton there as well. Eleven a.m. Monday, sharp. Byeeee.' And hung up.

'Now, Clancy, since you are free tonight, come back here at 6:00 sharp and we'll feed you.' Clancy understood an order when he heard one. 'Now, there's no room to stay here, so perhaps a motel in town.'

Clancy, 'That'll be the day. Ooh ha oohoo.' Buddy Holly was still popular. 'I'll unwrap me swag in the back of the ute. Me dog likes that too.'

Mary feared for their olfactory future of a big man's unwashed night in a swag with his dog for warmth. 'You can have first shower, now and in the morning. Here's a bath towel.'

Clancy understood an order when he heard one. He emerged from the shower quite a bit later, apologising, 'It's me beard.' That beard looked several shades brighter. 'Now, could I borrow a hair dryer?' Hair brushed all over, decked out in clean checked shirt, Clancy said he'd go into town and buy them all a drink. He'd take his time and be back by six. He was in for a surprise on his return.

Tom came along punctually at six. He did a double flip at the sight of the big man. Who wouldn't? In that confined colonial space with small rooms and low ceiling, he looked fresh descended down Jack's beanstalk.

'Tom Dooley, apprentice wine maker. You already know me rather too well.'

'Clancy O'Mee. We used to go to school together.'

'Never heard of Clancy O'Mee.'

'Try Eddie Murray for size. I was a bit smaller then. Still the same square chin though. I can't show you. My mother re-married. I adopted her name to make life simpler. Also, I took on my Christian name à la birth certificate. Now I'm authentic.'

'What are you doing here?'

Finn took over and delivered a lawyer's synopsis. He didn't mind Clancy talking, but feared Tom's endless interruptions. He carefully left out their coming Monday interview with the police, the existence of the notebook, and any mention of Carmel. He gazed the others into silence on the missing. They didn't need silencing.

Now no more business talk. 'Clancy, you might be interested in what Tom is doing with his life now.' He knew that henceforth he and Mary need not talk much for the rest of the evening. Just let Tom flow.

The guests left, totally exhausted by Tom's flow. When she

heard a groan of contentment as the dog lay its head on the red nest over Clancy's chest, she made one last call.

TwoBoots was not happy at being woken up at 11:00 p.m. on a Saturday night. Less still when Mary told him to drive to Moola next day. He settled a bit when she said that a 10:00 a.m. conference on Monday would let him off the hook once and for all.

Wilson to Merton, Over and Out

Wilson rang Merton at home as soon as that 'byeee' from his nemesis Mary Flamboya had subsided enough to clear his head. 'Will no one rid me of this troublesome bitch,' he said out loud enough for everybody up and down Thredbo Street to hear.

Merton bitched at Wilson, 'Can't I have just one Saturday off in peace?'

'No. Nor one Sunday neither. Monday we have to be in Moola for a ten o'clock conference with, wait for it, Finnbar Mahoney, Mary Flamboya, Carmel Blount, Freddy Ford and Clancy O'Mee. Why not Uncle Tom Cobbly and all!'

'So, Tom Dooley won't be there?'

'Mate, I was just using a figure of speech. Tom Dooley won't be there. Nor Bumfluff. Can't disagree with that. No case to answer. That bitch Mary stitched me up. Never gave me a chance to object.'

Merton, 'So what's new? You know when you've been stitched up by an expert. Now who the hell is Clancy O'Mee?'

'The only bloody person of interest we could not find and they could. The big man!

'And one last humiliation – they have the missing notebook! Spare me or I'll go spare! And another thing, that big Irishman is treating that notebook as privileged lawyer/client information and won't hand it over. We'd be able to subpoena it for the court case. Something tells me we'll never see it.'

'What do you mean?'

'I mean, that Mary's voice said it all without saying nothing. They are shaping up to show us on Monday that Tom Dooley, Freddy Ford, and Clancy O'Mee are all innocent. Now where do you reckon that leaves us? More than just red faces. Management in CIB Sydney will go off their faces. We've spent time, money, and human resources on this investigation. All for nought it would seem.

'I'll authorise overtime for us. They won't like it, but Mary has got them just as much by the short and curlies as us.'

Merton, 'Add in there the cost of my divorce.'

Wilson went on to say how lucky it was that they had both written up their reports as they went along. They would of course front the conference with pocket notebooks at the ready. It would look professional to have their A4 double-spaced properly bound typed records of interviews on the table. Don't give any start to Mary and Carmel.

'We need to know our reports inside out, I don't need to say. Mary and Carmel will probably have nothing in front of them, knowing them. The big Irishman will have a bloody big folder in front of him, of that we can be sure.

'Now, I know it's your son's birthday, but you can stay only until the Jolly Good Fellows are sung. Spend the rest of the time getting up to speed on your reports. I'll be doing the same here. Over and out.'

Sunday was like the Monte Carlo rally, in which competitors and their navigators from various countries run on various routes. They all converge for the last decisive stages around that fabled haven for the super wealthy.

Paxton and Wilson headed out from Jindabyne. Separate cars. Wilson would return to home base Sydney if he survived the conference.

Merton headed west from Sydney. He and Wilson would return in separate cars likewise.

Mary and Finnbar headed out from Mudgee, in the same car. Finn would stay at home afterwards. Mary would catch the train to Sydney and thence fly back home to Perth.

Carmel headed out from Sydney by train. This was a path well-trodden back in her PhD days. They seemed so long ago now.

Clancy O'Mee headed out from Mudgee, in his own 4X4, weighed down by red dust and his red four-legged faithful mate, fleas and all. He would return to the high country after a spot of 'roo shooting out west with his dog.

Paxton and Wilson and Merton would stay in some two-star flea-bitten motel or other that Mary had recommended.

TwoBoots had to make his own arrangements, forewarned where the detectives would be staying. TwoBoots headed out from Merimbula on his own. He would return home a relieved man, or so he hoped.

Clancy would unroll his swag in the back of his 4X4 parked in Finn's large back yard. Mary made sure Clancy had a good hot shower that night. She deliberately forbade him morning ablutions.

Finn lived in a big house. Mary and Carmel would have a bedroom each. And a bathroom too. Neither had been there before. They were in for a surprise at the quantity and quality of Aboriginal art that Finn had hung all around.

Dooley, blissfully unaware, would sleep on in Tom's cabin.

Showdown

Eight people all at once were a challenge to the facilities of Mahoney & Geeves. Or at least that's the impression that they wanted to give. They could easily have opened the bifold doors and properly socially distanced the attendees. No, Mary wanted to make the cops feel a bit off balance.

If they were all crammed in, 'their' side could overlook the reports of Wilson, Merton and Paxton, thanks to Clancy's altitude and proximity. Head of conference Finn could not be inconvenienced so. Mary and Carmel had no notes whatsoever. Nor Freddy Ford nor Clancy O'Mee. It would be off-putting to the police side to see the 'opposition' so confident.

Suck it up, thought Mary as they arranged themselves shoulder to shoulder, elbows tucked in.

Finn had no chance to say a word before Wilson sought to assert some sort of hierarchy in favour of the authorities. 'I really must object to the seating arrangements. You've got Mary, me, Paxton and this big man here on one side. There's no reason to split me from all of my men.'

Mary sweetly said, 'Sorry about that. We weren't thinking.'

As if, thought Wilson. But what could he say? Mary swapped places with Merton. Objection sustained. That put Mary and Carmel together, facing the police. Nothing like passive menace, especially of the Mary/Carmel variety.

It still left Clancy next to Paxton. Worse than having Mary and

Carmel facing you had to be a giant looking over your shoulder. And he stunk of wet kelpie and bulldust. But what could Wilson do about it? Clancy looked like he could stand on his own two size fourteens. It wouldn't do for the police to admit discomfort enough to have him moved. Where to? Meanwhile, Carmel would be a comfort to TwoBoots. They knew each other quite well from high school days.

Two women and two men against three men. No need to guess where the advantage lay.

Clancy had shoulders so big that they had their own time zones. This meant that Paxton had to squeeze closer to Wilson. Not only did that invade Wilson's personal space, it also had the effect of preventing them from fully opening their folders. They had to tilt the folder on one side or the other, depending on which side they were trying to consult.

Finn opened proceedings. Seeing as how the conference was being held in his boardroom, Wilson could hardly object. Also, Finn occupied the only accessible head of table position. The other end was too close to the wall to fit a chair. Mary's dimple said it all.

Finn, 'Thank you all for making this very important conference. There have been lots of interviews here in Moola, with the Brittens in Boolaba, with Carmel in Sydney, and Mary in Jindabyne. I have attended most but not all of them. There's no need for more interviews, and it's quite premature for any charges to be laid. That much is clear.

'We certainly don't have the answers as to who the guilty party or parties might be for horse theft. We will for the 'murder'.

'Let me be quite clear, by the end of this conference, we will show beyond all reasonable doubt who the innocent parties are. We will show that Freddy Ford, and Clancy O'Mee have committed no crime.

'Everybody already agrees that Tom Dooley and Adam Yates need no further investigation. Bumfluff is illiterate, and Tom had for a long time been moving from town to town. While he was elsewhere, crimes continued. Including the presumed murder of Martin.

'We have acquainted ourselves with all records of interviews conducted by DI Wilson, DS Merton, and Sergeant Paxton. Is there anything you would want to add to records of interviews, or any new material you have? I am aware that you interviewed Freddy Ford just this Friday last. I have not personally seen that record of interview.'

Wilson, clearly not in charge, a state of affairs to which he was by now only too accustomed, meekly said, 'That interview with TwoBoots alongside his lawyer Smith ended up with what we thought was a revelation. That is, until we learned that you were in possession of the actual notebook. Now it would appear that you know more than us, even though TwoBoots was marvellous in assisting with our inquiries.'

'That's correct,' said Finn. 'That notebook is client-privileged information until such time as it is clear that my clients have no case to answer. That might be as soon as today. Meanwhile I am happy to discuss anything at all about the notebook, which is locked up in my safe. Ask away.'

Wilson did not lean backwards or forwards, no show either of confidence or aggression. 'I'll consult my report here. It summarises where I think that notebook may lead the investigation.'

He started by tilting the folder up from the right, to render page one readable as he leaned to the left. It put him uncomfortably closer to the smell of bulldust and wet kelpie. *It must be hell for Paxton*, passed through his mind, but not for long. It didn't take all that long for partial conclusions to reveal themselves from between the lines as he read, evident first to Mary and Carmel. This, in spite of the guarded language used in the police report, which was often ambiguous, deliberately, in coppers' bureaucratese. That language now served no purpose, given the 'defence' had the original source document, the notebook.

Furthermore, Wilson wasn't to know that Clancy O'Mee and TwoBoots would change everything. Their roles would resolve the story that appeared in TwoBoots' handwriting.

TwoBoots had told Wilson that he used code for everything. Wilson hoped that Finn could not understand all the code in TwoBoots' notebook. Fat chance. Mary and Carmel had already deciphered it with ease.

Wilson, 'Freddy Ford here started to keep detailed notes early on. Just as soon as he felt he was being set up as an alibi for someone who was committing something, somewhere else, away from the O'Hanlon place.

'He started using code, just in case the notes fell into the wrong hands.

'Specifically, he thought that the big man was up to no good. That had to be. Why else was the big man there every sale day? His notes detail just what animals were going to the saleyards, and where from. We always thought that 'BM' was a name. At interview, we learned that it meant 'big man'. That's when we believed Freddy that he had no idea of the big bugger's name.

'The notes show there was no pattern to when Herbie Benninger and Adam Yates, I mean Bumfluff, were there. That let them off the hook in our eyes. What really got us was that Tom Dooley was on Martin's payroll. Freddy never did know, or he would have noted it. We still don't really know. We didn't believe Tom when he said that it was for weed control. For that you need a proper worker, not a shyster like Tom.

'The final mystery was Martin getting crooker and crooker, to use Freddy's language. The fact that he writes up notes about it tells us that he wasn't involved. If he was, he'd hardly be writing about it.

'And Tom was busy with his shitty little crimes in other places. Not guilty.

'Sergeant Paxton might want to add something. He was primarily looking into horse theft. Did a darned good job too, I might say.'

Paxton, 'I was approached by a grazier who reported six stolen horses. I followed up with the driver of the truck, who else was there that day, what did they know, and it just seemed like the thief had vanished into thin air. No clues at all.

'Then I dug around. Martin O'Hanlon had done time for exactly the same scam. Two years earlier. I went carefully through all the evidence. Martin couldn't have done it. The prosecution was too eager for a conviction. Justice didn't matter. It's not a proud day for policing, I'm sad to have to admit.

'I've interviewed everyone, barring Clancy O'Mee here. Nobody seemed to know his name. Naturally I started to think it had to be him. He was next on my list, but events have overtaken us. It did seem strange to me though that Clancy was there each and every sales day, yet the scams happened only twice.

'Why would anybody do that? That's why I have left him till last. I would have tracked him down no worries. He casts too big a shadow not to be noticed.

'So we had credible Freddy Ford, credible Tom Dooley laying out a petty crime trail from town to town, illiterate Adam Yates, and Clancy. This case was certainly a hard nut to crack. And that's only horse theft. Murder raises the stakes to a whole other level.

'The notebook was a great hope for us, when Freddy told us about it. It exonerated him, in my opinion. It focussed the spotlight on Clancy. He was a marked man you might say.'

Clancy thought, *I did well to be afraid. So glad I threw my lot in with Finn.*

Finn said he had an announcement to make for the benefit of the police party. 'Clancy O'Mee was born Edward Clancy Murray!' He let that sink in, to let Mary and Carmel luxuriate just a while in police discomfiture.

Who'd've chosen that timing? thought Wilson. *No prize for guessing.* He unbalanced visibly. Who noticed? Next question.

Then Finn invited Carmel to speak.

She said, 'I come at this from a completely different angle. I was working for Finnbar Mahoney as his articled clerk straight after graduating from law school. He asked for my help on the strangest of tasks. He had just completed the registration of a name change by deed poll, something that I would do, or a legal secretary would do. A principle needn't get involved except to sign papers.

'Now, Finn's a good operator, and his antennae were alerted because the request came in such a strange way. The original started way back in Jindabyne. By coincidence I was the receptionist with Lasseter & Co at the time. It was lodged by Jennifer O'Hanlon. The new name was to be Mary Flamboya.

'I recognised all this just as soon as Finn showed me. For what it was worth, I said that Jen had to be using some other alias, not Flamboya. To disappear she really had to cover her tracks.

'Finn and I confirmed that when it turned out that the document had been mailed from Adelaide, no return address, inside another envelope, no return address. And the registered name change was to be mailed to Poste Restante in Alice Springs.

'That first envelope was mailed to Mrs E Britten Boolaba. Turns out that she was my old classmate Eva Rumford. Small world, eh? Sergeant Paxton's clever sleuthing quickly led him to send DI Wilson to Boolaba to interview Bill Britten and Eva Britten.

'Then Wilson went to Mahoney & Geeves in Moola and met Finn for the first time. I believe they rather made a night of it. DI Wilson moved on to meet me in Sydney. I was rather free with my advice on how to track down Mary Flamboya. My apologies if I was teaching grandma how to suck eggs. No offence intended. I think we gained mutual respect through that experience.'

Her look invited Wilson's confirmation. He nodded, not with

any great show of enthusiasm. He also felt a little compromised that Finn and he 'had made a night of it'. *How did she know, for crying out loud?*

Then he remembered he had whistled a bar of an Irish air, and Carmel had immediately asked, 'Have you been drinking with Finnbar?'

'I told you, DI Wilson, what you needed to know. I didn't tell you all I knew.'

Why am I not surprised? thought Wilson.

'I knew we had to have a two-pronged approach. The detectives were one prong. Finn and I were the other. We placed a wishy-washy ad in the *Law Society Journal.* Lo and behold we got a reply from Brisbane that solved nothing but put us on the track to solving everything.

'It helped us identify that Perth was odds on Mary Flamboya's new town. At the same time we correctly surmised that she would be living under another alias. And we were correct in assuming that she would start a business, register a company, plus a holding company. Bingo each time!

'We also read the ad that the Sydney Flying Squad had placed in the national press about the scourge of horse rustling. We were less than impressed with that one.

'Finn here placed a discrete ad about the execution of Martin O'Hanlon's last will and testament, but only in *The West Australian.*

'Again, we reckoned that Mary Flamboya would answer in some shape or form. The form it took caught us completely by surprise. I think I have brought everyone here up to date what has been going on behind the scenes. I think Mary here should now take over.'

'I read the ad from the Flying Squad and phoned the number to confirm that it had to do with the Jindabyne happenings.

When Sydney answered and identified themselves, I hung up. Confirmation enough for me.

'Then I carefully read the notice about the will. There was a return phone number to call but no name. I put two and two together and came up with "Mahoney & Geeves", so I went to Moola Moola Yellow Pages and bingo! Right on.

'I sensed that it was only a matter of time before my whereabouts were uncovered. I was prepared and rang Mahoney & Geeves to engage them as my solicitor. I did not elaborate. Once in their office, I announced to Finn here that I was Mary Flamboya. The look on his face was priceless.

'We went to the Jindabyne police station, where I announced myself as both Mary Flamboya and Jennifer O'Hanlon. What a look on Sergeant Paxton's face! I think I may have left an impression with him after that day.' Not so much as an ironical smile, let alone a dimple. Eyes widened to briefly flash white all around each ebony iris. Paxton stayed glum.

'Carmel worked out how to uncover my alias. Must say, Carmel, that was clever work. Now, why couldn't grown men have worked that out? I announce now that I live in Perth as Mary Chiaprisi. At this stage of proceedings, that does not add to the sum total of human knowledge. It just helped me to cover my tracks back then, that's all.

'If you want to follow up on Carmel's advice on uncovering me, you'll find I own a company that has to do with coffee. I have committed no perjury in describing my occupation as "run a coffee shop".

'It's true, but in addition I import coffee machines from Italy, roast and wholesale beans, have a consultancy on coffee shop design, have a warehouse in Subiaco for bits and bobs that I sell to coffee shops, a gift shop, and finally, when I get back, a coffee museum attached to the warehouse in Subiaco.

'Oh, and I may have some additional income when I come to a

settlement with the New South Wales Police. I feel we've travelled too fast, got to the end too quickly. I wish this game could go on forever.'

Wilson could not help himself. 'Just put us out of our misery.'

'Right, I will. You may interview Eddie, I mean Clancy, here and now. Let him tell it in his own words.'

Big Clancy O'Mee took over, fiddling with his beard like it was his comfort rug. 'When TwoBoots turned up regular as clockwork, for no reason that I could work out, what was a man to think? I knew him from school, but he didn't recognise me. Can't blame him. I had a growth spurt. Good hormones for a beard. I liked that it meant no one could see what I was thinking.

'TwoBoots was a bit secretive at school, a hard box to open, so I didn't totally trust him. The way he was always pumping me for information. Then, when he thought nobody could see him, scribbling in a notebook. I was sure he was setting me up as an alibi for something he was doing elsewhere. A crooked something.

'So, there you have it, really. We each thought the other was up to no good and seeking to blame the other. Now, for the same reason that you concluded that Freddy Ford was not involved in crime, me too. I owe an apology to Freddy here, for thinking ill of him.'

'Me too,' was all that Freddy said, and offered a hand out to Clancy. They shook, and declared not quite their love, but 'no hard feelings'.

The three lawmen agreed that the men seated one in front of them, one looming alongside, were no longer persons of interest. Finn called in his receptionist and had her type out a statement that he dictated there and then. The partiep signed it without demur.

Handshakes all 'round.

Finn, 'We have worked out beyond plausible deniability who spread the rat poison! For that, we'll go back to Carmel.'

The Will

Carmel started speaking with a trained lawyer's caution, let alone one with a PhD. 'What I am about to say is without prejudice.' All three officers of the law knew what that meant. Mary Flamboya would be free to pursue the police for damages, if she so chose, after the revelations they now felt sure were about to emerge.

'There is a copy of the last will and testament of Martin O'Hanlon locked up in the safe back in Thredbo Street, Jindabyne. I also have read it, courtesy Mary Flamboya. Finn has that copy here with him. We can pass it around to confirm what I have to say about it. Mary can butt in at any time.

'The main body of the will was prepared by Lasseter and Co in Jindabyne. I happened to be there at the time, so I was aware. Martin was leaving his entire estate to Jennifer O'Hanlon, his wife.

'Quite normal. All the same, I asked Mary to see her copy, for the sake of thoroughness if Finn and I were to get anywhere with this strange case.

'Imagine my surprise when Mary's copy had a codicil attached, drawn up after I had gone to law school in Sydney. That codicil is crucial to this case of Martin's death.

'It includes Martin's mother as equal beneficiary in the event of his death. Now, I asked myself why any son would will something to his elderly mother. It goes against the natural order of things. Parents bury their children, not the other way around. This is every parent's fervent hope.

'I am judge's associate, and so cannot be seen to be working on any investigation that could potentially land in front of my boss at trial. Even if there is no chance of that happening, it is still the prudent policy of the judiciary to keep at very long arm's length.

'I relayed my concern to Finn for his action, whatever. Oh, and I nearly forgot, there is a second codicil, which I'll leave to Finn. That's all I have to say. I'd like to recuse myself from the rest of this conference. Finn, would you record that in the minutes of this meeting as per your tape recording?'

Paxton groaned inwardly. *I can't help feeling that I'm going to come out of this looking bad. Why had I not studied that will more carefully? I didn't so much as look through the codicils. Even now, I can't see the relevance of them. But then again, I don't have the luxury of a Carmel and a Mary on my side.*

He sought to protect himself with, 'We, the team investigating this very difficult case, had our hands full following up leads left, right and centre. Things have moved pretty fast over the last two weeks or so. Once we were done with Freddy Ford, we agreed that the will had to be examined by police lawyers. They are doing that as we speak.'

He felt rather proud of his statement. It was one hundred per cent accurate. He was very happy to have that recorded in the minutes.

With Carmel gone, the table arrangements looked decidedly lop-sided. Mary sweetly suggested, dimple free, that Clancy come over to the other side. That meant everybody had to get up, Finn to make way past the head of table, Merton, Wilson, and Paxton, in that order, to make way for Clancy.

Finn approved. This interruption purporting to favour the police team had the opposite effect. They were like putty in her hands. Wilson thought a silent thought, *Will no one rid me of this troublesome bitch?*

They did as they were bade.

Now their team had to face up to the piercing, red-surrounded green eyes of Clancy. And Clancy did as Mary had asked, 'Stare them down.' He looked like an Easter Island moai with luminous eyes. A thousand-yard stare. Frozen into stony hardness.

He added another distraction all his own. He leaned forward and sucked noisily on his beard. It put off the freshly showered coppers with their cheap aftershave. They had compensated for their bad taste by liberal splashes. They smelled like an aftershave factory. That still did not eliminate the smell of wet kelpie and bulldust emanating from the big one.

Mary slitted her eyes enough for everyone to notice, and held her 'gotcha' dimple for longer than was strictly necessary. Civilians one, coppers nil. Finn carried on as though nothing had happened. Luckily you can't write down a silent movie. Luckily it was indelibly imprinted in his mind.

'The second codicil is the critical part of solving this murder. It states, "Any beneficiary found guilty of a serious crime cannot draw benefit under the terms of this will."

'I have never seen the likes in my years as a lawyer. It smacks of a forgery. I have had that checked. It is no such. All the signatories to the codicil – Martin, witness, and solicitor – are genuine signatures. We have confirmed that the will and two codicils are also genuine.

'Try as I might, I cannot come up with a reason for that will not to be executed forthwith, after grant of probate of course. Mary, I am happy to tell you here and now that that is in progress. Rest easy. You and Martin held title as joint tenants. Your mother-in-law replaces Martin as per the will. When she passes, the property will be one hundred per cent yours, no legal expenses or stamp duty. That's the easy part. I think the police team can rest easy that they have been thorough and professional in their investigations, if sometimes over-enthusiastic shall we say.'

'Strike that last comment from the record,' ordered Wilson. Finn readily agreed, happy to be generous with a small victory. Mary thought, *Finally you are learning your lessons from me.*

Finn continued, 'That covers the letter of the law part. It gets us no closer to solving the mystery. It gives me no satisfaction that my client Mary Flamboya here has been cleared of any misdemeanour, more to the point.

'DI Wilson, do you want to comment?'

'We're not interested in misdemeanours. The murder investigation will continue. The only person of interest remaining is Mary Flamboya, formerly known as Jennifer O'Hanlon at the time that we believe the crime was committed. She had motive, opportunity and means. The latter is clear from the postmortem report. Her husband was poisoned with low dose strychnine over a protracted period. It's impossible to go past her as the perpetrator.'

Mary displayed no emotion at this direct accusation. Wilson back to his bullying best, forward lean and all. *I'll set you back in your chair*, vowed Mary.

Finn sought to clear the air with the investigators. 'I apologise unreservedly to the police team for any intrusion into police work. This was never my intention. In light of the unusual nature of this case, I felt I had to push the boundaries, let us say, in how I could afford protection to my client. So far this morning, I, Carmel, and Mary have revealed every step that we have taken. The written record will be clear that I have been ethical in my work.

'What comes next will, I believe, demonstrate beyond all reasonable doubt that Mary is no murderer. Shall we break for lunch? It will be convenient for both sides to confer. Back in one hour?'

Both parties went their separate ways.

There are no Winners

Lunch was five at one place, three at another. The police nosh was the more interesting affair.

Wilson, as the senior cop, opened up as usual. 'Jees, how did we get roped into this unequal contest? Those bloody women stitch us up, I think it's fair to say. And then that smooth Irishman manages to polish his halo as we wriggle and squirm, as though he has nothing to do with it. What do you guys think?'

Merton, 'From the minute I've let them speak, I've felt as though I've been done over by experts. I still think so. I'm resigned to it, unless you can tell us how to turn the tables.'

Paxton, 'My first encounter with Mary was when she fronted the police station. I've never told you this, but I've never felt so helpless. She gave me a right royal bollocking. I was shell shocked for a while afterwards. Then next day when DI Wilson and I were interviewing her, butter wouldn't melt.

'I can tell you, I was melted. And we both got the quiet, deadly going over. I have to take my hat off to her. What's she going to come up with this afternoon?'

Wilson again, 'I thought that Carmel Blount was the cleverest human I had ever met, that first time in judge's chambers. Not offensive or anything like that, just ever so sharp. Nothing got past her. She was helpful to a tee, but kept her cards close to her chest at the same time. Formidable.

'And then I felt the same about Eva Britten.'

Merton, 'Me too. She wasn't aggressive or offensive, different to Mary in that way, but she anticipated what I was going to say. Uncanny.'

Wilson, 'Let's just agree, then. We have been just so lucky to have rubbed shoulders with this trio. There is no shame in running second best to them.'

Clancy spoke first at the other lunch. 'Jees, but what a stroke of genius that you ordered me, Mary, not to shower this morning! And Paxton couldn't get away from me. Ha ha.

'Sucking on my beard was all my idea. Disgusting. I never do that normally.'

Mary, 'We'll do a whip around to fund your beard trim. You'll never have to suck it again. Disgusting. But brilliant.' The five of them could not stop laughing for five minutes.

Carmel, 'This whole unfortunate affair is falling right into our laps. We set the thing up but never knew that it would pan out this way. We have had a lot of luck with the timing of Freddy's interview, his confession about the notebook, Mary suddenly finding it in her handbag. On and on it goes.

'Mary, it shouldn't take you too long to wrap this up this afternoon. Champagnes are on me tonight.'

TwoBoots and Clancy, 'We don't know how you do it.'

Mary, 'It won't take long. It's a bit sad though that, in reality, there will be no winners.'

Denouement

The reassembled conference had a decidedly more relaxed air compared with the morning. Well, the five-a-side were more relaxed. The three-a-side were more, shall we say, resigned?

Finn opened up with hoping that everyone had enjoyed their lunch. His troupe – he avoided saying 'side' – certainly had. He hoped that Moola's best café at the bakery had done itself proud with the police. Without waiting for confirmation, he handed over to Mary.

Mary, 'It's my privilege to close proceedings of this conference. I can't begin to tell you how important it is to me. To the police, I offer congratulations on a job well done. At the end of my presentation, I'm sure you will see why. Right now you must be wondering what this bitch is on about.'

Wilson reddened ever so slightly. Only Mary noticed, and then only because she was watching him intently. Never had Wilson felt so under scrutiny.

Mary continued, 'Everybody here is well acquainted with my story. Up until now, each of you have had different points of view, most not favourable to me.

'Let me say it has not been easy for me. Forget that you may have gained the impression that I was guilty as hell. "Why else would she have run away?"

'I explained that to the investigators, and they have accepted that explanation, I believe.

'I also accept that that doesn't let me off the hook. If I were investigating my case, I would be doing exactly the same as them. I'm not here to tell them how to do their job. I am here to tell them how they can wrap it up. That's what my evidence will demonstrate. The police are welcome to accept it or not.'

Wison thought, *Jees, even when conceding defeat she manages to come out on top. Let's just hope there is no humble pie on the menu for us.*

'Now, to sum up my situation. It does not look good. But is is is, was is was, and I wouldn't change one word of it. Thus I rounded up my strays. Martin is poisoned slowly on my watch. What kind of carer is she?

'Well, he was also poisoned under the noses of men who were around. I couldn't figure how they couldn't have seen Martin grow sicker bit by bit. The police have now accepted that no man was involved in the poisoning.

'What twigged me to what actually happened is when I discovered that Tom Dooley was on the payroll. I found this out from the books that I kept for the farm.

'Martin flew off the handle when I mentioned it. "None of your bloody business." I never asked again but my antennae were up. Sure as shooting, Tom did no visible work for his money. And he turned up from time to time, not every sale day. Other men did. And the police have accepted that they had legitimate reason. Not guilty, in other words.

'I found out, never mind how, that there was a codicil to Martin's last will and testament. Martin's mother is equal beneficiary to me. Strange enough on its own. Downright menacing when read in conjunction with codicil 1 – nobody with a serious criminal charge can benefit.

'That's when the penny dropped. He was going to frame me for some serious crime. Tom Dooley was being paid just to bear witness against me when the time came. Where in the hell did that leave me? Up the creek without a paddle, that's where.

'Try as I might, I couldn't figure out what he might do. At first, I thought that the horse scam was it. No way, because I was kept so far away from the running of the farm that I could not do it.

'Then it hit me like a thunderclap. Martin was self-dosing on rat poison! As he got slowly sicker, at some stage Tom Dooley was expected to go to the police and swear on a stack of bibles that it was me.

'Tom must have gone to water. He was a petty crim, and did not want to be involved in the strangest false witness you have ever heard of. He shot through to another town, and then town after town after he had worn out his welcomes. His shitty little trail provided the perfect alibi. No wonder he continued down that path. To stop would have halted his alibi.

'What happened next is kind of poetic justice. Martin was found guilty of a horse scam that he didn't and couldn't have done. He gets sent down for six months, two off for good behaviour.

'It had dire, unintended consequences for Martin. He was going to get himself treated for strychnine poisoning. He had misread how much the human body could tolerate. Outside, he could perhaps have been saved. Inside, and it was his own death warrant. I didn't know, because I never intended to visit the bastard.

'His plot was simple. Blame me for his slow poisoning, have me convicted, with Tom Dooley's connivance, lock me up for a very long time, change his will, take up with some floosie, game over. I get out of gaol after eight years or so, life ruined, no money, no prospects.

'The rest of my story is history.

'Now, I don't think that the police can pin anything on Tom. He will deny it. It is plausible that he did pull weeds, if highly unlikely. And it's no good asking me to testify against Tom. It was purely circumstantial. I couldn't swear under oath that Tom was going to conspire with Martin for Martin's self-harm. It's just too far out there.

'And in any event, Tom did not and could not have administered the rat poison to an unwilling Martin. How, for crying out loud? He was only there for a few hours on the morning of sales, and even then irregularly.

'Now, DI Wilson, you can see why I think your team were doing a good investigative job. Nobody could come up with a plot like the one I have just outlined. Nobody.

'Finally, you might be thinking, "Why didn't she get Martin to a doctor?"

'Well, I did raise it with my doctor. You can go and check. The doctor is still practicing in Jindabyne and will confirm what I have just told you. Any questions?'

The investigators were knocked for six. Wilson pleaded for more time, much more time, for them to respond. That might take weeks, to talk it out with his seniors and police lawyers. He thought that this was a case for the ages. Mary, Carmel and Finn agreed. Clancy and Freddy were flabbergasted, and said so. From the plots of men of evil, pure evil.

Mary brought the assemblage near to tears with what she said next, 'Why can't I trade the things I can't remember for the things I can't forget?

Loose Ends

Finn's conference room descended into a low murmur, like in the movie theatres just before they tell you to return your empty glasses, turn off your mobile phones, and shhhh, no talking.

Once heart rates settled back to near normal, Wilson quietly asked to be heard on the last matter before they could dismiss. 'Where does that leave us with horse scams and dodgy brands?'

Finn, 'I have no idea. Mary didn't steal or scam. I would have to confer with my advisors before I could come up with any hypothesis.'

Carmel, 'I never was any fan of horses. Not my area of law. I didn't even know that horse brands had to be registered. Until now that is.'

Freddy Ford, 'There were dodgy horse brands involved. We couldn't do anything about it. If the paperwork matched the beast, that was that. Martin instructed us to accept them at face value. If a complaint was registered, then the Flying Squad would be called in. I always took that to be a bit of a tall story, because I wouldn't know what the Flying Squad looked like.'

Clancy O'Mee, 'Our stock grazed quite remotely. One road in, same road out. There was a locked gate. It has never been broken into, in all the years that I worked there. My boss does everything by the book.'

Mary, 'I don't give a stuff. My life is elsewhere, and I have no idea what dodges Martin practised. For me, once the paperwork came in, and the monies reconciled, Martin left me alone. Even the better-than-taxman's audit that I did when a new cooking recipe came from the saleyards, could shed no light.

'It had to be Martin that did the scams. There is no other plausible culprit. And with Martin dead and buried, there is no other plausible witness. I say to the law, "Just put it down to experience."

The parties split. Two to Sydney in separate cars; one to Jindabyne. One to Merimbula. One to the back of beyond for 'roo shooting, then back to deep in the Snowy Mountains. With lots of 'roo tails for his dog.

Two to Finnbar's. Mary via Finn's thence by the train to Sydney and Perth. Carmel via train to Sydney by herself.

Epilogue

'October's last,

I'll fly back home

rolling down winding way

And all I've got's a pocket full

of flowers on my grave

But now summer is gone

I remember it best

Back in the good old world

I remember when,

she held my hand

and we walked home alone in the rain

how pretty her mouth, how soft her hair

nothing can be the same

and there's a rose upon her breast

where I long to lay my head

and her hair was so yellow

and the wine was so red

Back in the good old world'

Tom Waits

Bachelor Finnbar this time was dry-eyed. He would give Carmel Blount-Mahoney the gift of Blarney.

Carmel slipped her hand into Finn's. She laid her head on his shoulder.

Young glamorous Mary, with her arrow and bow, smiled her knowing smile, the one without the dimple. Her man would get the same treatment.

But she knew that there would be no wedding waltz for her. Mr and Mrs Martinelli would have as their guest Signor Tarantella.

Shawline Publishing Group Pty Ltd
www.shawlinepublishing.com.au

SHAWLINE
PUBLISHING
GROUP

More great Shawline titles can be found by scanning the QR code below.
New titles also available through Books@Home Pty Ltd.
Subscribe today at www.booksathome.com.au or scan the QR code below.

Ingram Content Group UK Ltd.
Milton Keynes UK
UKHW041034270723
425881UK00004B/69

9 781922 993472